Karen Jennings

Upturned Earth

Holland Park Press London

Published by Holland Park Press 2019

First Edition

A CIP catalogue record for this book is available from The British Library.

ISBN 978-1-907320-91-0

Cover designed by Reactive Graphics

Printed and bound by
CPI Group (UK) Ltd, Croydon CR0 4YY

www.hollandparkpress.co.uk

Upturned Earth is set in Namaqualand, the copper mining district of the Cape Colony, during the winter of 1886.

William Hull arrives at the town to take up the position of magistrate, a position that no one else wanted to accept because of the bleak and depressing locale. He finds that the town is run by the Cape Copper Mining Company and the despotic mine superintendent, Townsend. Meanwhile, Molefi Noki, a Xhosa mining labourer, is intent on finding his brother who was sent to jail for drunkenness and has yet to be released.

Set against the background of a diverse community, made up of white immigrants, indigenous people and descendants of Dutch men and native women, we are given insight into the daily life of a mining town and the exploitation of workers, harsh working conditions and deep-seated corruption that began with the start of commercial mining in South Africa in the 1850s and which continue until now.

While *Upturned Earth* is a novel about the past, its concerns are very much founded in the present.

A prosperous land, a land where you will eat bread without stint, a land whose stones are iron and from whose hills you will dig copper.

Deuteronomy 8:9

Even the soil here is not like back home...

Mineworker 1*

*Peter Alexander, Luke Sinwell, Thapelo Lekgowa, Botsang Mmope, Bongani Xezwi. 2013. *Marikana: A View from the Mountain and a Case to Answer.* Johannesburg: Jacana, p. 75.

COPPER MINING DISTRICT, NAMAQUALAND,
CAPE COLONY
WINTER, 1886

Four men filled the cylindrical basket-lift, their shoulders wedging them tightly against its inner rim. Above them crossbars were just low enough to jostle hats as the basket tilted to left and right along its journey from the deck onto the pier of Port Nolloth.

Already several others had travelled in this way. A lady in the dyed garments of a mourner, her face veiled, hands gloved, and her two-year-old son whose mouth was crusted over with cold sores, his lips a scabbed O that cracked and bled when he licked them. Next onto the basket-lift had been an elderly man and his white bulldog. They had entered one by one, the dog leading its master across the threshold of the small entryway, its door hinged with strips of leather that creaked stiffly when it was shut behind them. As the basket rose, the dog became many-tongued, panting from all angles through small gaps in the wicker. The man whistled a half-tune. Above, sea birds flew.

Most of the other passengers, young men to the last, had simply hoisted themselves up the perpendicular rope ladder that connected pier to ship. They were ill-featured, scrawny, mouths swollen with red gums and rotting teeth. They carried with them lice and a plague of boils, as well as various rashes and itches that became common property before too long. Now they stood nearby, jeering at the men in the basket, eyeing all directions at once. A few had approached the lady, dallying with oaths and gestures as her son watched. One of these men said enough to cause the woman to turn her head away, gasping into the knuckled ball of a handkerchief. Meanwhile, another group was by turns spitting into the water and calling to the near-naked blacks to 'unload the sorry bitch', 'Get that luggage off her, we've got places to go!'

Within the basket, two of the four men were holding William Edward Hull beneath his arms. His legs had buckled as soon as the whistle blew, signalling for the donkey to commence pulling the chain and raise the basket-lift off the deck of the *Namaqua*. Ill at the motion, Hull's head hung downwards, his face hot, his mouth filling with a rush of saliva in anticipation of vomiting. Moisture dripped from his nostrils across the pale hairs of his moustache, over cracked lips, into his beard. He groaned, nodding, so that his wet face patted his chest in several places, leaving textured marks of damp. Then his head was wrenched back, his scalp tight under a rough hand, and his neck pushed up until his nose almost touched the crossbars.

'Breathe deep,' his neighbour said, holding Hull's head in place. 'Take in that sea air.'

Eyes closed, he inhaled through his nostrils, their wet insides sucking with each inhalation, popping as he exhaled. Then his mouth barked open and he began to burp and gulp, aware all the while of the stench of his breath in the faces of the other men. Six days he had suffered this sickness, or perhaps five. He did not know. He longed for land and the steady earth beneath his feet. Dirt or rock or sand. It didn't matter which.

There had been no sea legs gained by Hull since leaving Cape Town. In the weeks before his departure, the west coast had been ravaged by winter storms that had continued to plague the *Namaqua* on her short journey to Port Nolloth. Only a fortnight previously the *Veronique*, anchored at the Port to collect copper ore, had been lost in a storm, and two of her neighbours badly damaged. But the *Namaqua* was a small steamship and little affected by the weather. It rose and fell in the waves, carried great heights and depths as easily as a cork stopper. In this rolling tub Hull had lain in his cabin, sick with the movement, sweating and gagging, too ill to blink or swallow. He heard only the rain and waves around him and the sound of his luggage, which he had not secured, sliding along the floor and bumping into the cabin walls. Beside his bunk a wooden pail had been placed by a boy in trousers that were torn below the knees. He spoke in an Irish accent so thick that it wasn't until moments later that Hull had been able to decipher: 'You see that you puke in this, not on the floor.' He had, but storm-pitching toppled the bucket, and the roaming luggage smeared its contents across the cabin until the air was all acid and stomach.

Kept indoors by the weather, youths loitered in the corridor, knocking on Hull's cabin door, playing at heaving and retching. 'We'll put ya out of ya misery,' they called. 'O'erboard with ya!'

They were unschooled, these men who were not able to sign their names or even to read them, and travelled the colonies working as farmhands, stevedores, miners or wagon drivers. Names were given to them according to their origins or passions, such as Down Under Tom or Whiskey Pete. They were christened too by scars or afflictions, acts of strength, the colour of their hair, the shape of their ears and noses, losing the name of their birth as they sailed or rode or walked their way from home. There was nothing finicky in the women they bedded and by whom they fathered bastards in many colours. Wages

13

they drank, while friendships and animosities alike were ended with punches and knife-cuts in brawls that spilled from pubs into streets and alleys. Theirs was an existence of violence, of dirt, of work and drink. They had no time for weakness.

Eventually it had been the captain who prescribed rum and water to ease Hull's suffering. This concoction, more rum than water, administered hourly by the ragged-trousered boy, kept him in a constant state of intoxication. Nauseated, his face seemingly absent with drunkenness so that his whole head began to feel like a pair of large unblinking eyes, he lay below deck. Once, the door was left open while the boy held Hull's head and poured the liquid into his mouth. It spilled onto his beard, ran down his chest. He spluttered, saliva forming a thread between his jaws. Outside, the woman with the child was passing. She paused and turned her veiled face in his direction. He saw himself as she might: a lunatic under care, torso exposed, with a soiled shirt riding deep into his armpits. He was unable to cover himself, unable to appear any less than a madman. Hull reached a hand out to her, opened his mouth to say something, though he knew not what. The woman moved away, ushering her son in front of her.

When he was alone, apparitions in loincloths emerged before him, carrying weapons and the freshly slaughtered carcasses of a variety of creatures, imagined or extinct. They approached him with war cries, as though launching an assault. He attempted to distance himself from them, but could not, his sole movements being the rolling of his eyes, and three fingers on his right hand gripping the sheet on which he lay. Before him they threatened, cutting the heads off the dead beasts, aiming spears and arrows at his face. 'Go away!' he cried, though all that sounded was a sigh.

Then the tattered boy returned with another dose of rum, and Hull fell asleep mid-drink, waking hours later in the dark, the ship still, the seas calm around her. He climbed out of bed on all fours and left the cabin on his knees, pulling himself along the corridor's railings and up the stairs until he was upon deck, two-footed. A cold breeze blew under a sky, starlit and broad. He clutched at the gunwale as the sweat on his forehead and back cooled.

He heard still the wails of savages and could not help a fumbled touch of neck and chest to determine whether he had been struck by one of their arrows. Even now in the open quiet air he could imagine them, walking on the water, coming towards him, mouths wide with battle, their naked bodies red from slaughter. He started when he heard a footfall behind him, turning rapidly, his hands midway to his throat, a cry muffled on his tongue.

It was the woman, walking still veiled despite the dark.

'Forgive me, you startled me! I thought I was alone here,' he said.

'I am only taking the air for a few moments.'

'As am I. I have not travelled by sea before. I find that it does not agree with me.'

The woman pointed out at the darkness with her gloved hand. 'Tomorrow, if all goes well, we should be able to see the Kamiesberge ahead of us. It is not much further after that.'

'Indeed? You know this place? This Namaqualand?'

'Some of it.'

'I am new to it entirely,' he said. 'I am to be the new magistrate at Springbokfontein.'

'I wish you luck then.'

'Shall I need it so very much, do you think? Is it so terribly savage?'

She lifted her palms slightly. 'What does anyone care for savagery if there is copper in those mountains? That is as much as a place needs to make people call it home. As far as I have been able to see, they care little for anything else.'

'You do not find the mining life agreeable?'

She stood silent for a moment, before taking a step

15

back. 'If you will excuse me, I had intended to come upon deck only briefly, and I fear that I have stayed too long. My son will be wanting me. Goodnight.'

'Yes, of course. Goodnight.'

Hull remained where he was, looking out at the dark water lapping all around him. Again he tasted rum and sighed, resting his forehead on the cold hardness of the gunwale. He thought, as he had for weeks already, that he had been a fool. It was nothing but bloody ignorance for him to have imagined that a clerk at the age of 28 would be singled out above all others to be Residential Magistrate of an area as vast as Namaqualand.

Weak-willed, forgetful, Hull was a poor employee. He did as he was told, yet somehow was never able to fulfil the chores of the position with the same success that his colleagues did. He confused cases, misfiled documents, knocked over inkwells. Often he arrived late or left early, and could regularly be found looking out of the window at the view of Table Mountain and its slopes of grey and green. When he wrote, it was illegible, on papers stained with the fawn-coloured dirt that somehow never left his pockets, that worked its way under his fingernails and formed half-moons of shadow on his hands. He carried the droppings of animals folded in handkerchiefs, kept pink newborns warm in his hat.

Now he was here on a silent dark sea, soon to arrive in a land of a hundred thousand wild men. He would hold a position that, only after papers had been signed and hands had been shaken, he discovered had been offered to him because no other man would take it. For a moment he squared his shoulders. He would be firm. Punishment would be meted out. The law would be laid down. He would be admired for his diligence. He stooped again, head in hands. He was nothing more than a convict travelling to his prison. A prison lifeless, the stones of its walls, the bars of its windows, comprised of grain upon grain of sand.

The following day, in rough waters, the *Namaqua*

docked at Port Nolloth, port of the Cape Copper Mining Company. Dropped onto the pier by the basket-lift, Hull was left to tremble on his knees with nothing more from his shipboard companions than a pat on the back and a finger pointed in the direction of the hotel.

There was no one to assist Hull at the hotel's reception. Only a dim and small lobby in which two faded armchairs and a table bearing a vase of browning paper flowers gathered dust. A tortoiseshell cat was asleep on one of the chairs, but opened an eye to watch as Hull seated himself on the other. His head ached and the nausea of the past days remained heavy in his stomach and throat. Beneath him the land still appeared to be moving, and he felt at all times about to be upended. He sat with a sigh and allowed his feet to slide forward on the sand-laden carpet. In this posture, crotch thrust upwards, torso shrunk into the seat, he rested with eyes shut.

'Would that be you, Mr Hull?'

He shuffled hastily into a sitting position and looked up at a man in his shirtsleeves. He wore his thinning grey hair scraped back and had a white bush of beard that yellowed around his mouth. His spectacles were so marked with water spots that Hull wondered how he could see through them.

'Ah yes,' Hull answered. 'My luggage is still at the pier. There is a porter, I assume.'

'Indeed, there is,' replied the man as he leaned over the cat and ruffled its fur. 'You won't find him now, however. He will be collecting supplies from the ship. But you needn't worry. This is a small town, as they say, and the porter will know what is yours. He will bring it along in good time.'

'Very well.' Hull paused a minute, waiting for the man to offer to show him to his room, but he continued playing with the cat, which had by now rolled over to show a white belly. 'I have been very ill,' Hull said. 'I should like to lie down.'

'The landlord will be here shortly. He will be supervising down at the pier this minute.'

'You are not he?'

'Ha! Not I, sir. I am your predecessor at Springbok-fontein. Reginald Tweed.'

'Oh, Mr Tweed!' Hull jumped up and shook hands with the man. 'I am very pleased to meet you, sir. My apologies; I am not well. I have been ill.'

'Yes, so I've heard,' Tweed said, and the yellow of his beard twitched.

'You have retired, I believe.'

'Yes, blast it! Twenty-five years in this godforsaken country. I'm returning to Southampton, the place of my birth, you know, to live out my last days amongst decent people.'

'I see.'

Tweed grunted lightly and looked around at the reception desk before turning to Hull. 'Mr Baker, the landlord, will be an hour or more yet. I may as well give you a tour of the town.'

Hull paled. 'I've not been well, sir. I cannot go outside. You are very kind, but I've not been well.'

'Nonsense, Mr Hull. You will have to be tougher than that if you plan to stay here. Come along.'

Outside the wind was blowing, sand grains flying into Hull's beard and teeth.

'You learn to like the taste of sand out here,' Tweed said, wiping strands of hair back from his forehead with a flat hand. 'It gets to a point where you don't feel quite right without a grain or two in your mouth. After all, it's what the miners eat, isn't it?'

At the pier a string of partly clad natives was unloading the *Namaqua*. It seemed the whole town had come to watch. They stood waving handkerchiefs and calling out, 'Are there oranges? Have you seen oranges?' 'Did the post come?' A few women were among the group, their children with them. They shielded their eyes with their hands and stood waiting, at times whispering. The children jumped up and down, pointed, laughed. A man as broad as a doorway shouted, 'Where's the blasted Cape Smoke? Where is it? There's people what needs their liquor.' Further out to sea two ships loaded with ore to carry to Swansea rolled lightly on the waves, and nearby, on a small black-stoned island, the fat bodies of seals rested, their wet fur dulling under the afternoon sun.

On land, iron-roofed buildings of wood, single storeys all, resembled one another in design and size. Each was as sand-blasted and mouldering as the next. Tweed waved his left hand. 'Private dwellings there.' Then he waved his right hand at a row of buildings nestled between mounds of drifting sand. 'Customs house, CCMC store, workshops, engine shed.' At the last, five natives with spades were digging the structure out from a sand dune that was beginning to consume it. Little progress was made, the wind lifting the sand off the spades and blowing it back onto the building.

Beyond lay a dreary settlement of huts and shacks fashioned together from sacks and skins and thin pieces of wood. From where he stood, Hull could make out dark figures in the openings of the shacks, some bent over fires, others standing, their heads cut from view. Outside the huts children ran naked.

'That's the native settlement,' Tweed said. 'Some work here loading ore onto the ships. Mostly they are just loiterers, waiting for work at the Okiep mine.'

'Why not live at Okiep then?' Hull asked, sliding and sinking with each step in the loose sand of the street. Beside him Tweed walked lightly, unhindered despite his age.

'Okiep is CCMC owned. Most of these places are, but Okiep is still a private town. It's the headquarters, you see, so you have to get Company permission to stay there, even for one night, even you or me. It was the same at Springbokfontein a decade or two ago before the main works moved to Okiep.'

Hull scanned the settlement. Shanties lay in unpatterned heaps, climbing over one another up the heights of the surrounding sand dunes and down the further sides. Home upon home appeared to be absorbed by the sand, breathing brown and black from their submersion. Here a dune grew, there it scattered, shifting and rising, reshaped daily. Natives sat amongst it all, too fatigued by idleness to move. Sand blew over their feet. It covered their hair, filled their ears.

Hull lifted a handkerchief to his nose. Even at this distance the smell of the settlement was rank, its odour brought nearer by the wind. 'There are so many of them,' he said. 'Surely they won't all get work?'

'There are many, many more of them waiting for you at Springbokfontein. Ten thousand of them, I'd say. But you will see, they need only wait a while. Replacements are always needed at Okiep. Two to three are buried a week over there.'

'A week, you say? Surely not?'

'It's the smelter. Pollutes it all – air, water, food. There's no escaping it. Copper must be got and some will die.' Glancing at his companion's frown, he added, 'It's the way of the mines, Mr Hull. There's no getting around it, so you may as well accept it and think of it no more. You are a magistrate, remember that, not a visitor from a benevolent society. Leave charitable deeds to spinsters and the clergy, that is my advice to you.'

Behind them, at the pier, the broad man had received his shipment of Cape Smoke. He bellowed instructions at a row of natives who hoisted the casks onto their shoulders and carried them to a donkey cart. Already the wheels of the cart were sinking into the sand under the weight. Once every tub had been loaded, he reached up and took a single cask from the top of the stack. This he tossed at one of the natives. It was their pay, and the labourers began to squabble over it before the two donkeys could be whipped enough to pull the heavy cart through the soft sand.

The following morning a thick fog had descended on the port town. Windows framed views of grey. Small icicles, fine as hairs, latticed the corners of the glass. Hull waited outside for the train. He could not see beyond a few yards. It was bitterly cold. He hopped from foot to foot, wishing he had worn something more substantial than the light suit that he had been advised by a Cape Town tailor would be essential out in the copper lands. He had not considered seasons, had not thought that his post might be surrounded by anything beyond hard and brutal semi-desert.

There appeared to be no other passengers waiting, though he could hear voices not far from where he stood. 'Hello?' he called. 'I say, is there anybody there?'

He was answered by silence. Half a minute later the voices began again. 'Hello,' he repeated, turning in all directions. 'Could you tell me whether this is where I wait for the train?'

This time there might have been titters, but still no reply, and Hull thought that he should have had the foresight to reach into his pocket and give the hotel porter some coins to wait by his side in this blindness. Alone, the cold crawled deeper into his bones. He jumped up and down, his hands folded into his armpits so that he looked comical, chicken-like. He jogged forward five yards, keeping the rail at his side lest he lose it in the fog, then back again, before turning round and advancing another five, puffing out white breath.

All at once a mule loomed out of the thickness before him. It was followed by another and another until a wheeled box drew level with him, driven by two men. 'My good man,' he called in alarm, 'you can't stop here, there's a train arriving any minute.'

The driver and his partner guffawed, answered by a score or more laughs coming through the mist. 'My good man,' the driver mimicked, 'this is the train!'

Further laughter sounded beside the tracks. All along the rails, stretching back towards the pier, stood the mule train. It was composed of thirty open boxes for carrying ore, each pair pulled by six mules, but a few singles, reserved for passengers, pulled by three. Two drivers were assigned to each mule-set. The front one blew a whistle and his partner called hoarsely, 'All aboard for Okiep.'

Hull watched in dismay as a dozen people stepped out of the fog, one of them the woman with the young son from the boat. Along the track several of the drivers called, 'Passengers here!' and helped the travellers to their seats. Each of these individuals had heard Hull's panicked call, each had heard his to-ing and fro-ing, the silly whining hum as he jumped and hopped, and none had spoken out to him.

'You're in this carriage, Mr Magistrate, reserved just for you and Mrs McBride and little master George there,' said the front muleteer, cocking his head at the canopied box-cart he was driving. The woman and her son were already seated, and Hull hesitated as he looked up at them.

'Come on now, sir, you're keeping everyone waiting,' the driver said, taking Hull round the waist as though he were a lady, while the other man pulled him up into the box.

'Mr Hull had better sit here where Georgie is,' the woman said as Hull was directed towards a dusty purple cushion. 'He is not a good traveller; he will become ill if placed facing the rear.'

Again hands were upon him, and he was set down beside the woman, who now held the boy on her lap. Another whistle blew, and with a jolt they were off, jogging into the murk.

Though fog-ridden, the journey to Five-mile Station, where the mules were changed, was smooth over flat land. After that followed the tedious slog from station to station at different distances and heights from one another. Some were five or eight miles apart, others no more than two or three. So slow was their progress that passengers were able to get off from time to time and walk beside the train to stretch their legs. Little master George, whose mouth was now covered in a deep brown unguent, begged to be let down. For half a mile he walked beside a whip-carrying native in a shabby pair of trousers. The boy shouted up to his mother, drawing her attention to each step he took, to the rocks that lay around, to the hills that were formed where piles of these had accumulated. With his child's language he named clouds and sky, sun, a bird on the wing. Hull fell asleep to this babbling, waking later at a small station, no more than shed and stable, and again at others where the drivers barked the stops as passengers came and went to places with names gibberished: Oograbies, Abbevlaack, Anenous, Ootoop.

Then, at last, rising slowly out of the plains, the ascent up to Klipfontein Station began. By now it was late afternoon, and Hull's ears and the back of his neck were crimsoned by sun, despite the tasselled canopy that drooped with heat above them. For hours there had not been a sound but the clop-clopping of the mules, the murmur of driver talking to driver. Nothing to see, nothing to do. Only a hot sun, a dreadful sun, and hooves on gravel, on and on. Many times during the day Hull had been tempted, as other passengers had done, to remove his jacket that now felt heavy as a blanket, but it was the woman beside him that kept him from doing so. It would be improper to expose himself to her in that way. He sweated and reddened, drinking liberally of the water offered to him by the muleteer.

Propriety too was what had kept him from conversing with her. He knew her name through the driver only, and, though they had spoken briefly onboard ship, they had never been formally introduced. He sat awkwardly, determining to keep silent. But a bit of dust in his throat caused him to cough a little, and she turned to him in expectation, thinking he wished to speak.

'You are visiting the area, Mrs McBride?' he said at last.

'I am returning to my parents, to my childhood home.'

'I see.'

'I left when I married, and did not imagine that I would ever return. But now it is scarcely six years and I am returning, as a widow.'

'You have my deepest sympathies, Mrs McBride. To lose a husband, when you are so young...'

'I may be young, but my husband was not. However, it was illness that killed him, not age. I was ill too, for a long time, and when I woke in my sickbed some weeks later, I was told of his death. There was a telegram to say I was to return to my parents when I was well enough to do so.'

'You are not pleased to be returning, I imagine, under these circumstances.'

'Would anyone be?'

'No, I think not.'

She turned her face away, resting her chin on the head of the boy, and did not speak to Hull again that day other than a soft 'goodnight' in response to his own when they reached the night's stop at the hotel on the plateau.

He stumbled from the box, dusty and shivering in a cold that was sudden, raw. He ate alone at a table in the large dining room, tasting little of the dishes placed before him: tortoise soup, white ants with onion, Namaqua pigeon pasties. He did not see the woman and boy amongst the other diners. In the night he slept fitfully, moving, always moving, but never reaching his destination.

The following day they set off again in the morning dark. Mrs McBride and her son dozed beside Hull, and he considered that they had likely slept as poorly as he had himself. Yet he found himself unable to nod off, not when he saw the steepness of the descent falling away beneath them, and the expression of the second driver as he handled the brakes, causing metal to squeal and the mules to whip their heads. Hull imagined them stumbling, his own body falling, the broken corpse lying at the bottom of the precipice and nobody bothering to retrieve it. It would become the territory of scavengers, his limbs torn apart, torso burrowed into. Bones might remain, white as chalk, while shreds of his clothes would line animal lairs in the bouldered mountains all around.

The hours sunned and shadowed, the landscape flattening out before them. Then 'We're here,' he heard Mrs McBride whisper, and Hull looked up at a smoking chimney stack, towering over a village gloomy with the dirt of it. As they drove up through the outskirts, Hull observed that Okiep was different from the Port, made so by the presence of stone buildings rather than wood. Some of these, small cottages, had a green bush or two ornamenting their front doorways. He was compelled to pull a handkerchief from his pocket and cover his nose and mouth, his eyes burning in the smoke-heavy air. The bulk of the town – roads, hillocks, plains – was black with slag, though in places the black was tinged blue-green with samplings of oxidised gravel and stone that lay around.

A tall man in a broad-brimmed hat and sack suit of the kind popular in the previous decade approached the carriage as it came to a stop. The suit was marked by wet patches under the arms and stains of orange dirt at the cuffs and ankles. Despite his height, the man was wide and stout, his neck and chin greasy with the hair oil that he used on his moustache. He helped Mrs McBride from the carriage, kissed her cheek through the veil. 'Your mother will be glad to have you home, Iris.'

Then he bent to the boy, who had been lifted down by a driver, and said, 'So, this is the little chap then. Doesn't look too well, does he? Now, Georgie, not a word of greeting for your old grandfather, hey?'

The boy hid his face in Mrs McBride's skirts, and she placed a hand on his head, saying, 'He is tired, Father. The journey was long. But here is Mr Hull for you.'

'Ah yes,' he said, turning, 'here you are at last, Mr Hull. Welcome to our little bit of heaven.' He waved at the slag heaps. 'The name's Townsend, Charles. I'm superintendent here, representative of the CCMC board. I see you have been keeping my daughter company.'

'Oh yes,' said Hull, 'but I did not realise that Mrs McBride, I mean to say that I had not known the pleasure—'

'How did you find the journey?'

'Surprising, I would say.' He looked across to where the mules were being unharnessed.

'It won't be like that for long. Soon, within a few months, I hope, we will have a steam engine here. It will change things, by Jove. Yes, change!'

Townsend gestured at some navvies nearby and they began to unload Hull's luggage and place it in a horse and cart. Mrs McBride and George had walked a little distance from them. She was pointing out something for the boy to see, and Hull followed the line of her finger, seeing no more than rubble and slag. But then a small bird, brown and dun, flew up from the blackness, and he thought with disappointment that it must have been that.

'Basjan will see you to Springbokfontein,' Townsend was saying, his hand on Hull's elbow as he led him towards the waiting cart and driver. 'Nice little home for you there. No rent. That's a formality we dispense with here.'

Hull shook his head. 'Sir, I assure you that my salary makes allowance for rent.'

'Allowance? Nonsense! Now, employees are not allowed to keep their own horses or vehicles or whatnot. Them's the rules and that's how it is. But there's a well-stocked stable at Springbokfontein and you say the word and borrow what you like. Horse, cart, mule. Anything.'

As Hull climbed onto the cart, he spoke with some anxiety, 'Mr Townsend, I am not an employee of the mine—'

'Free postage for you at the P.O.,' Townsend rushed on. 'Then of course all your fuel, gas, water, all that is supplied and paid for by us.'

'Please, Mr Townsend, I believe there has been a misunderstanding. I'm a magistrate, not a Cape Copper Mining Company employee. I am here to uphold the law and the great name of Her Majesty the Queen.'

Townsend leaned close to Hull, droplets of oil glistening between the hairs of his moustache. 'Don't be a fool. Out here there is no Queen, only a King, and that King is the Company. You'll do as you're told, boy. Out here all bodies bow to the King.'

The driver whipped the horses and they took off, carrying Hull towards his new home.

Faint against the glare, objects loomed in the heat. What looked like homesteads half a mile away faltered into rocks within yards. Earth and sky had rotated so that sand moved above him. Beneath, he trod on a perpetual midday, his shoes chafing and melted by the sand until nothing remained of them, and he went barefoot. Once, squinting, he saw what appeared to be a herd of springbok line up before him. As one the beasts paused, tossed their heads, before wavering and collapsing until revealing a solitary animal. It snorted, and Molefi Noki watched as it ran off, knee-deep in a watery haze.

He was alone, returning to the copper mines from his village in the Idutywa Reserve in the Transkei Territory on the eastern flank of the country. It was the first time in his five years in the mines that he had made the journey home and back again on his own. In the past there had been a group of them, 30-strong, returning twice a year to their villages to sow or reap their maize crops. Together on the long journey, the men would hunt, carry enough water to share, or scout for more when it was necessary. But in recent years the CCMC had been shutting down some of the mines, most notably those in the vicinity of Nababeep, neighbour to Springbokfontein. They were worked out, the Company said. Yet they had said the same before, closing the Blue Mine at Springbokfontein for several years in the previous decade, the same mine that was now seam-rich and in which Noki laboured six days a week. Nevertheless, the number of copper miners from Idutywa Reserve had declined until all that remained were Noki and his brother, Anele. As it was, Noki alone had been given permission to visit his home that winter. The mine boss, Reid, was becoming less willing to have his workers absent themselves for planting and harvesting, begrudging them any life outside the mines.

Some time into the journey to his village, Noki had fallen in with a group of seven men returning from the diamond mines in the middle of the country, and together

29

they had camped around fires after a day of trudging. The diamond miners enjoyed the freedom of their homeward journey, for in Kimberley they were kept in compounds which they were not allowed to leave without permission. Each morning they rose within guarded fences, walked in orderly lines to the mines where they blasted and drilled the rock, faced invasive searches for diamonds they might have secreted about their person, before coming back to the compound where they ate and slept, piled together like hunting dogs, with no sign of a woman for months at a time.

They were full of news that gold had been found in the north, in the Boer Republic, at a place called the Witwatersrand, or as some called it, the Rand. It was said that in its rock there was more gold than a thousand men, even a hundred thousand, could dig out in a lifetime. And as had happened with copper and diamonds before, the earth with its contents was beckoning. Already men were making their way to the Rand from across the globe. White men with hair the colour of fire, Zulu, Herero, strange slit-eyed Chinese, turbaned Indians, and men with skin like midnight. All of these steadily marching to the gold mines to take a part of the earth for themselves.

A few of these hopefuls they saw in their ox-wagons and horse-drawn carriages. But the way north was not easy and Noki and his companions found more than one ox left to die. Even once a carcass of a horse and that of its rider, both of them eyeless, their entrails eaten by scavengers. One of the men from the diamond mines picked up the hat that lay near the remains and put it on his head. 'Now I am a gentleman,' he said. They had all laughed, but secretly they envied the man his new possession, wishing they had seen it first. Another laid claim to the rider's boots, but finding them too small for himself, sold them to a slighter man for the sum of five beers to be paid on their first Saturday night back at the compound. Because, despite their hatred of the mines, they would return. The colony offered its natives little other option for a chance at survival, nor any other means to pay the taxes that the government claimed each native owed to the motherland.

After several days of travelling together, the men parted ways, as the diamond miners were going to Gcalekaland, southeast of Noki's village. Since they had last been home it had been annexed by the British, they had heard, and it was now renamed Willowvale in order to appeal to white farmers. By its renaming the white man would know that the savage land had been tamed.

Lulama was in labour when Noki arrived at his village; a month too early for the child he had left inside her at planting time. It was her voice that he heard as he approached, the sounds of her screams coming from the confinement hut. This was always her way with giving birth. The child coming too early, Lulama sick for all the months that it lived inside her. So it had been at the mines when she had worked there with the other wives and children, sorting through the rubble of crushed rock for those containing copper ore. Weak with child, she had fainted too often, done too little sorting, had been sent from the line and told not to return. Then she lay in their hut made of sacks, taking nothing but sweet water that came from the Company well. It was distributed by a man pushing a rolvaatjie and cost more than Noki could easily afford, but there were no springs or wells that were not company owned that did not contain brak water. Sometimes Noki gathered condensation on goat skins stretched out at night. But that small amount was not enough for the sick woman who sweated and panted day after day, begging for fresh water. Eventually the baby had come, three months early, grey with the death that was already upon it.

After the burial, Lulama had pleaded to get her place back at the sorting area, but her weakness was known and she was not wanted. Nor could she gain employment at the Namaqua Copper Company. An agreement between the two companies meant that they did not employ one another's cast-offs. Eventually Noki had chosen to send her back to the village, paying a man and his wife who were returning to Fenguland to go out of their way and take Lulama to the doorstep of his family hut before they went on to their own village. By then she was once again with child, so ill that the Fengu and his wife had to take turns in carrying her on their backs.

Noki had given Lulama a ragful of coins and instructions to see a sangoma when she arrived home. This she did, paying to have the witchcraft lifted from her womb. It had been successful, for a girl was born, alive, two months early and very thin. When he had returned home for the sowing, Noki performed the imbeleko ritual, taking a goat and holding it by its horns in front of the doorway, addressing mother, child and ancestors. He had chosen a sturdy, large goat so that the blanket made from its hide might make his daughter strong, might let her live.

It was early morning yet as he reached the village, the sun hardly warm enough to clear the winter mist. Several old men were sitting on rocks around a fire, wrapped in blankets of cowhide. Behind them trees grew tall and strong, the grass long and green as phosphorescence to Noki's eyes after the dun semi-desert. Orange spears flowered from the aloes that dotted the bright valley and surrounding mountains. All was damp and alive.

'Good morning, fathers,' he greeted them, stepping forward to warm his hands at the fire.

'You are welcome,' they murmured, as though it had not been months since they had last seen him. They barely looked up. The sight of one of their sons in trousers and shirt arriving home from the mines was not a new one.

'I'm glad to be returning for the maize at such a good time,' he said, gesturing at the hut. 'That's my wife in there.'

One of the old men, his eyes rheumy, turned to Noki and shook his head. 'You are mistaken, my son. It's not a good time. Not for maize, not for anything. Didn't you see the fields as you came? Have you been underground so long that you have gone blind?'

'It's true,' said another, lifting his arms wide so that the grey curls on his chest could be seen. 'All this is now the white man's. Their farms are everywhere. We have some land, but do we have our rivers and streams?'

A third man, older than the rest, spat into the fire. 'We all belong to the colony now.'

Noki let the old men speak. It was nothing they had not said before. They talked this way each day whether anyone was there to listen or not.

The man with the grey chest hair pointed at Noki. 'A man needs a strong wife. A man who is not here to look after his fields must have an even stronger wife. It is time for you to marry again. There are women in this village who are waiting for a husband.'

Noki wiped his brow, licked his dry lips, said, 'Thank you, father, for your advice.'

For some time the confinement hut had been silent, only the movement of women in and out of the doorway indicating that something was occurring inside. Now the jagged cry of his wife was taken up again, and Noki's stomach turned at the agony of it. He stood and looked towards the structure. Toddlers and young children were loitering near the hut, watching silently until a woman came out and chased them away, her hands heavy with a wet rag. As they retreated from her, one of the children fell. She sat on the ground, crying. A girl, some years older, picked her up beneath her armpits, dragging her to a patch of dirt under a flat-crown tree where the children now congregated. The older girl began to draw shapes in the dirt with a stick, and the children bent down, picking up stones in preparation for a game.

Noki observed each child, unable to recognise himself in any of them. 'Fathers,' he said, 'which of those children is my Fezeka?'

The man with the milky eyes coughed. 'I cannot see that far, but I can tell you that none of those children is your daughter. She died many months ago.'

'Died? And no one thought to send word?'

'How could we? We're old men and women here. Which of us can walk all the way to the mines to deliver a message?'

'Still, it would have been better to know.'

The oldest of the men spoke. 'In your heart you already knew.'

He sat on the ground outside the hut that he shared with his wife when he was home. He had not bothered to enter, knowing what it held and what it did not. He watched a neighbour-woman grinding millet grains, the small stalks of germination having dried to shreds in the sun. She ground in the old way, rock on rock. There was a baby on her back, wrapped in place with a goatskin. The woman was on her knees, rolling a smooth stone over the millet on a flat rock, her activity lulling the child to sleep. It could not have belonged to her, she was too old, her breasts brushing the ground as she worked. Over and over she rolled backwards and forwards until the millet had been ground into a fine paste. Of this she took a portion, measured by sight, and added it to a large clay pot of water. In several days' time there would be beer. As the woman stilled, her work complete, the baby woke, crying loudly and wetly. The woman dipped a rag in goat's milk and let the baby suck on it.

The confinement hut had quieted again. Now a woman exited and came to where Noki sat. 'Twins,' she said. 'Two boys, but one of them is dead.'

Into the small grave was lowered first the living twin, before being replaced by the corpse of the brother. A part of each twin was dead. A part of each was alive. His head shaved in mourning, Noki watched as the surviving child was returned to the confinement hut where its mother was waiting. Later over a fire made from live coals and isifutho twigs, Lulama would grab the baby by its legs and arms, waving it through the smoke to give it strength and health.

By day he toiled in the field, bringing in the maize. There were no other young men in the village. Those who had not already been employed as migrant labourers had recently left for the Rand. Those from the diamond mines had not yet returned. Perhaps they had not been given permission to leave the compounds, or perhaps they had been delayed. They were at the mercy of their overseers, being set free at a whim, or detained by similar impulse. But the crop could not wait, and so in the village it was the women and children who were left to do the reaping. Hardly more than infants, few were tall enough to reach the cobs with ease; they grew tired, listless, wandered away despite the threat of beatings. Beside them, the aged pulled and basketed with gnarled hands, working slowly, very slowly, but never stopping. The maize was needed and there was no other way.

By night Noki slept alone, knowing that it would be weeks before his wife and child could leave their confinement. He would not see them until his next return, by which time the child might already have the ability to recognise strangers from others. No doubt the child would scream when set in his father's arms. He would close his eyes so as not to see the face of a man who smelled of other places, who carried the soil of a different world with him. So it had been with Noki's own father whom he had seen briefly, anxiously, in the same way when he returned from the diamond mines each year. That stranger in his white man's clothes who brought gifts of umbrellas and holed paper fans. Who spoke of places and things that Noki had no notion of. As a child he had wished the man gone with each of his visits, and one year he did not return. The wish was fulfilled, with memory reducing the stranger to a broken-rimmed hat and hands as rough as stone.

Some nights Noki drank beer with Lukholo, who six months previously had been sacked at the diamond mines for concealing a diamond in a cut in his thigh. Discovered, he was beaten and sent away in nothing but rags, the wound suppurating. By now it had healed and Lukholo had grown fat, enjoying the life of an idle man. He cradled his belly like a pregnant woman. 'Half a year is all it takes to turn a skeleton into a man,' he said. He rubbed his hand over its round hardness. 'You cannot be a man on the mines. All day being called a boy. Me, a man with five children, I am a boy.'

Noki gulped twice from the bowl and passed it to Lukholo. 'It is their way, bhuti. Being called a boy does not make you a boy.' Then he tilted his head and pointed at the other's belly. 'A man must take care of his family. You can't sit idle while your family starves.'

Lukholo wiped his mouth with the back of his hand and shuffled his feet. 'I'm tired, bhuti. I feel old. How many years is it since I threw myself into the mines? I was buried there. This is my corpse you see before you.'

Noki eyed him as he drank. 'It's a healthy corpse.'

'Heeeeee,' Lukholo said, holding his belly again. 'Yes, I can feel it coming back to life.'

'You laugh, but what have you to laugh at? Five children and two wives to feed, while you sit there with your fat stomach.' Why should any man have a strong wife, healthy children and days of leisure when others were labouring and struggling? Why should any man have more than others? 'A man who is healthy should work.'

Lukholo frowned at his companion. He put his hands on his knees as though about to rise, but instead he grunted and leaned forward. 'I'm telling you that I've had enough. What sort of life is it living underground so that we can be paid less than nothing, where we beg to be allowed to come home once-twice a year to see our family? Never sleeping enough, never eating enough, fighting over the torn shirt that a white man has thrown away.'

Noki's head fuzzed and shrank; he had drunk too much. He was angry, he knew that, but he could no longer precisely remember the source of his anger. 'The mines...' he began, forgetting what he had wanted to say. It was them, perhaps, that he was angry about. But the mines were so far away. Maybe that was what he had been saying, that a man travels long distances, a man lives underground. He does what he must, in the mines, in the fields. He does everything that he can. But Noki did not continue with his speech. Not now, tired as he was. Tired deep into his bones, his teeth, his jaw, down through all his fingers and toes. No part of him free from it. He felt his eyes close, felt himself falling into a sleep of aching toil, of dust and metal, of stale air and sweat. It was a sleep of darkness. And far away the whispering, whispering promise of daylight.

He took his leave early, waking the wife of his cousin before dawn, giving her messages to pass on to the men who had not yet returned. He placed money in her hand, for Lulama, and mentioned names he had chosen for the boy. She cried, said he ought to wait a little, let her prepare food for him at least, but he shook his head, said there was no time. He passed the grey ash of several fires, patted the head of a tethered goat, swung his pack upon his shoulders and left the village, his road for some way enclosed by the stubble left after the harvest.

In the late afternoon Lukholo caught up with him. The fat man was sweating and out of breath, his face pale from the hills he had just climbed. 'Wait, bhuti, wait!' he gasped, then spat, breathed, spat again.

'It would be better for you to go to the gold mines,' Noki said. 'There is little work at the copper mines.'

'No,' Lukholo waved a hand, still breathing heavily. He wiped his forehead. 'I came to tell you that the child died.'

Noki said nothing. The men sat on their haunches smoking a pipe, looking out at the green and yellow valley below where a white farmer was hammering planks into a new home.

Two days of dull, naked scenery behind him, Hull was taken aback by the industry of Springbokfontein as he was driven up to the Residency. A mountain of slag announced the presence of the mine behind it, and upon that mountain men, women and children moved. They appeared to be adding to the heap, coming and going with sacks of rubble. An engine operating some or other contrivance sounded away from view, so that the whole of the valleyed town echoed with its roar. Shouts could be heard over the rumbling as the workers communicated queries and instructions to one another. Mule-drawn cocopans, similar to those that had comprised the train, slogged in the direction of Okiep under the whips of natives in an assortment of cast-off clothing. A collar studded in place on the neck of a shirtless boy. Trousers patched with goatskin or the flattened silk of a cravat on the rear and knees. White men walked unshaven, their beards matted and dusty, their moustaches unoiled. Hair curled greasily at their shoulders or stood upright over their foreheads where hands sodden with labour had pushed stray locks out of the way.

The main road, stretching from the Residency to the mine, passed buildings that were ugly, cheaply built. Orange dust, blown from the direction of the mine, layered the streets, filming windows and roofs. Mounds of it duned around the mine, haphazard, irregular in size. Among the fouled buildings, Hull could make out a store, post office, stone church and a long line of stables beyond. Some of the buildings that might once have been lodgings appeared to have been abandoned. Their walls had collapsed inward, their windows, doors and roofs missing.

He alighted from the carriage and saw a man move out of the shadow of a doorway some hundred yards away and begin to make his way towards the magistrate. The man walked with a pronounced limp, his hips rolling uneasily in the sand-deepened street.

'Mr Hull,' he said as he neared, and Hull noticed that

the man's shoulders were strangely hunched up so that they brushed his earlobes. 'I'm Thomas Genricks. The jailer.' He pointed to the building that he had come from.

Hull smiled and shook the rough hand that was held out to him. 'Mr Genricks, how good to meet you. I have been advised by Mr Tweed that you will be of some help to me.'

'At your service,' he said, brushing hair from his eyes and squinting up at the magistrate. 'You can rely on me, sir. I been here long enough to know the ropes. Oh yes, I know it all, top to bottom. Was a miner first, for seven years, then came the accident, me leg you see,' he nodded down at the limb, 'so they put me to the jail these two years.'

He gave the magistrate the key to the Residency and invited him to enter, saying that he and the driver would bring the luggage. The building was no different from the others. It had a wooden exterior and roof of tin that glowed orange in the light from the lowering sun. Outside, the sand had been raked into neat lines, undisturbed by footprints. Inside, it was quite dark, the late sun not bright enough to reach all corners. But there was enough light to see the basics. Two bedrooms, a kitchen, dining room and sitting room. A door in the passageway led into the Magistracy, in which were Hull's chambers and office, complete with benches for when he held court, and beyond it a waiting room with more benches. The whole had come furnished, with items so old and dark and heavy that he could not imagine them having made the same impossible journey that he had just completed.

Trunks clubbering across wooden flooring caused Hull to hasten outside in order to pay the driver for his trouble, but the fellow was already some distance away, heading back to Okiep, a quarter-moon pale in the sky above him. Despite the twilight, Hull could still perceive bustle on the rubble masses of the mine. Even now the growl of machinery persisted, and he wondered how far into the night this activity would continue to noise. He had exited

41

the building through the waiting room door and now walked round the outside towards the Residency's front entrance. To either side of it were shrubs. He bent down to touch them, feeling the dry leaves crumbling between his fingers.

'He give up watering 'em when he found out he were retiring,' Genricks said from the doorway. 'Not that they grew much anyway, but I didn't want to be the one what pulled 'em out. Thought as you might have green fingers, sir.'

'That was very thoughtful of you Genricks, but there is no life left in them, I'm afraid.'

'I'll pull 'em out tomorrow then. Now, I begun unpacking and there's stew on the stove and if you don't mind taking a seat inside and passing me your shoes, I'll just give 'em a polish for you so's you can start the morrow fresh.'

'But where is the servant? I asked that a servant be engaged.'

'No need for that, sir. I do it all. Happy to.'

'But surely it's not your job?'

'As I say, I'm happy to do it. Now, come along inside, sir, it's getting cold out here.'

Hull followed the limping man indoors where lamps had been lit and curtains drawn against the twilight. Already the jailer had found amongst Hull's trunks some possessions that he felt might ornament the rooms. Several books were angled on a bedroom shelf, a cut-glass ashtray rested on a side table in the sitting room. Trinkets and baubles, collected over a lifetime of stasis, had been placed as though their significance was understood. By Genricks' hands, the dead, stale place had somehow come to life.

'Very good, Genricks. It feels like home already.'

'Thankee, sir,' Genricks beamed, putting out his hands for the shoes.

Hull woke the following morning well after sunrise. He dressed in the robe and slippers that Genricks had laid out for him the previous evening and went through to the kitchen where he found the jailer busying himself in preparing breakfast.

'Morning, sir. Sleep well?'

'Oh yes, I slept the sleep of the dead. Though it was some time before the motion of that journey left me. I was riding for hours yet.'

'So it can be.' He led the magistrate into the dining room. On the table were a fresh loaf of bread wrapped in cloth, a pat of butter, prickly-pear jam, a pot of tea and a plate of small steaks. 'Springbok,' he said, pointing at the plate. 'Fresh shot, just yesterday.'

Hull sat down to eat, while behind him the jailer waited, pre-empting his movements by passing butter, cutting bread, removing plates. He shadowed the magistrate so intently that at each bite he moved his own mouth in mimicry, while at his side his fingers echoed the motion of cutting, of stirring, of lifting a teacup to his lips.

'I suppose I shall inspect the jail today,' Hull said at last.

'Don't trouble yourself, sir. There ain't many prisoners on the books. Eighteen, all in fine health.'

'It is no trouble. It is my job to inspect the prison, the guards and criminal inhabitants of the cells.'

'Your wish, sir. I only want to save you time. They's all out just now in any event.' He picked up an empty dish and took it through to the kitchen, leaving the magistrate to call after him, 'Out? In what way do you mean they are out?'

'Prisoners and guards, sir. Out collecting wood,' came Genricks' voice from the doorway.

Hull turned to look at him. 'Wood? What for, in heaven's name?'

'Smelter, sir. Ain't no one told you the Company owns the jail?'

Hull wiped his mouth and stood up. 'No. I was not informed of that fact.'

The two men walked out of the house together. Outside, where the dead bushes had been the night before, there now ran neatly raked lines that seemed to grow from the building itself and draw it out towards the peeling white fence. Hull looked at the threaded sand, wondering whether Genricks had left the Residency at all or whether he had been there the entire night, working silently to repair the indentations made by his arrival.

It was no distance to the jail, and with each of those hundred yards Genricks' limp seemed to trouble him less, his shoulders to slacken away from his ears. A coloured guard slumped at the door, chewing on the nails of his left hand, spitting out the results. But he straightened when he saw the jailer approach, and saluted neatly when introduced as Cloete, a descendant of the two brothers who had worked the farm Melkboschkuil before selling it to the copper companies, watching afterwards as the land on which they had tried to foster goats through drought and cold for almost a decade was turned inside out.

Genricks showed the magistrate to his office and pointed out the tidy desk, orderly shelves of books and notes. A faded sketch of a lamb sleeping beside a pool ornamented a brown-coloured wall.

Hull frowned. 'What is that terrible smell?'

'Manure, sir,' Genricks said, reaching up to one of the shelves and lifting a ledger from it.

'Manure?'

'Cow manure. Walls and floor. For insulation and insects. We done it fresh in preparation for your arrival, so's all would be neat for you. Smell'll be gone in a day or two.' He offered the magistrate a seat in a ladder-back chair and handed him the ledger.

'Thank you, Genricks. I will look at this later. For the moment, I would like to continue with my inspection of the building.'

Genricks cleared his throat, looked at his pocket watch and shuffled papers on the smooth-rubbed desk. Then he led Hull into a dark passage at the back of his office and mumbled, 'Cells right, yards left.' He made to turn back, but Hull stopped him with, 'Some light please, Mr Genricks.'

The jailer slowly patted his pockets and brought out a box of matches with which he scrabbled until one of them ignited and was used to light a lamp hanging on a nail nearby. The magistrate took the lamp from him. He threw its beam over the ceiling, wall and floor, noticing the smoothened surfaces of cow dung everywhere.

'Very good. Now the cells, please.'

'Ain't got the keys on me.'

'Well, fetch them, man. What are you waiting for?'

Genricks walked away from the light, back into his office. He stayed away some time, though Hull could discern no movement coming from that room and was under the impression that he was standing stock-still. Some minutes later the jailer returned, passing both the first and second cells. He opened the third and let Hull enter. It was empty, bare and clean. Hull exited and then waited. The jailer did not move.

'I wish to inspect each cell, Genricks.'

'I tell you, sir, it ain't necessary.'

'Now see here, Genricks—'

As he spoke, the jailer's name was echoed by a call coming from the direction of the office. A middle-aged man stood in the doorway. 'Ah, there you are, Genricks.'

'Mr Hull, this here is Dr Fox, the Company doctor,' Genricks said. 'Dr Fox, Mr Hull's the new magistrate.'

The doctor stepped forward with his hand out. 'Of course! Yes, I heard you had arrived. Welcome, Mr Hull, and please accept my apologies for this interruption. I have stopped by to leave some tincture for one of the prisoners. He has a slight cough. It's normal in miners, I'm afraid. And then they all smoke so much. Weak lungs are the result.' He turned to Genricks. 'I left it in your office in the usual place.'

'Mr Hull was just about to make a 'spection,' the jailer said.

'Oh good, yes, very good,' cried Fox, putting his hand on Hull's shoulder and steering him towards the office. 'But you know there is simply no need. I'm here twice a week, if not more. Lots of brawls, you know. I'm forever sewing the blighters up. It's a lovely life they have here in prison. They grow fat and lazy and get better food than I have at home, you know. Now, Mr Hull, if you'll forgive my impertinence, I've ridden here from Okiep and am parched. Any chance of a cup of tea at the Residency?'

'I am afraid—'

'Excellent! Lead the way, Mr Hull, lead the way,' he said, pushing the magistrate ahead of him out into the street.

Hull fumbled the descent from doorstep to sand and knocked into the other man, his knee twisting beneath him, causing him to give a little cry and grimace at the discomfort.

Fox caught him by the elbow. 'Steady there! Are you all right? Yes, I'm afraid it will take a while for you to adjust to this cursed sand after the cobbled luxury of the city. Come along then, we had better make it a pint, I think. Doctor's prescription.'

Hull stammered, 'It is not yet eleven.'

'Indeed, but it will be a very light one, I assure you. Tea will not suffice to wash down this dust lodged in my throat. And let us not forget your knee. That will need some rest now.'

He showed Hull across the street to a wooden building outside of which a white-haired woman sat idling. She was smoking a pipe and glared at the approaching men.

'All well, Nellie?' Fox greeted her.

In response she spat into the dirt.

The street outside the pub held litterings of bottles, both smashed and whole, cork stoppers, the tail ends of hand-rolled cigarettes, globs of chewed tobacco and small balls of sand where spit had dried. A shirt crumpled in the street not far off, and to the right someone had abandoned a shoe – a working man's boot, its sole gaping away from the leather uppers.

'It's open, if you're waiting for an invitation,' Nellie barked. 'Haven't closed yet. Been working all night.'

'That's the way, Nellie old girl.'

She humphed and pulled on her pipe.

They entered the cool dark building. As Hull adjusted to the gloom and the smell of stale smoke, Fox said, 'Nellie came out here in the late fifties with the copper boom. All the way from Natal dressed as a man to preserve her dignity, whatever she had left of it. She's been a barmaid here ever since, though she owns the place now. Has done for years.'

A slapdash wooden counter, laden with tumblers and tin cups, fronted the length of the left-hand wall. It was backed by shelves of bottles and drinking vessels of various shapes and sizes and materials. On the floor beneath the counter, barrels stood, bellies rounding outwards in invitation. All the rest of the large room was taken up by small tables and chairs, some of them no more than crates or tree stumps, and towards the back stood a billiard table with a green surface dusted to grey. The walls of the pub might once have been whitewashed, but now they were stained yellow and were peeling. Several horned skulls were mounted on nails. The bone was flaking, so that the skulls were oftentimes akilter, skewed by loss into unnatural masks.

At the counter, Fox thumped the wood so that the glasses tinkled. 'Alfred!' he called and a coloured man leapt up from where he had been sleeping on the floor. He rubbed his eyes with the foreknuckles of each hand and then glared across the wood at the two men, his nostrils wide. The magistrate paused in his breathing, sickened briefly by the reek of sweat and alcohol that came from the man.

'Two pints,' Fox said, and Alfred bent to tap them from a barrel.

'Actually,' Hull said quickly, 'a ginger ale for me, if you have it.'

'We don't,' the man replied, putting two tin mugs on the counter.

They carried the mugs over to a nearby table so stained with circles from wet glasses that the impression was of an artwork done with intent. It was sticky and thick with its previous users and Hull had to jerk hard to lift the mug from its surface, spilling beer on his sleeve.

'Ah, very good,' Fox said, taking a long drink and smacking his lips. 'We don't have all the things you might be used to out here, but we have enough to get along pretty well.'

In one of the corners a man was asleep, his head on a table, hands and arms hanging down. A native half-heartedly wiped the table top around him with a dirty rag.

Hull took a small sip from his beer and was about to return it to the table before changing his mind, simply holding the mug in his hand, allowing his wrist to rest on his thigh.

'Now tell me, Mr Hull, how are you finding it?'

'Well, I have only just arrived, so I couldn't say.' He paused. 'Genricks has been very helpful.'

'Ah yes, a good man that. Very reliable, you know.'

Hull shifted in his seat and carefully moved the beer to his other hand. 'I did wonder. You see, he seemed reluctant to let me inspect the jail.'

Fox nodded and placed his empty mug on the table. 'Proud man. Very proud of his jail and prisoners. He feels they're his, in a way. He doesn't want to share, you see.'

'Well, that won't do at all.'

'You must understand. We are out here in the middle of nowhere, very little in the way of civilisation. Maddening heat and dust, bitter cold in winter. We've all developed peculiarities, you know. Poor Genricks has nothing but his jail. I believe you could say the prisoners are his only friends. There's no more than two people in this town who would greet him in the street. Is it any wonder he's protective of what to him is his home and family?'

'Yes, I can make sense of it now.'

'Alfred!' Fox called, causing the man to jump up again and bring another beer, his bare feet kicking up sawdust as he walked. 'As I was saying, Mr Hull, we all cultivate our peculiarities out here. It is kinder and easier to turn a blind eye to them.'

'I imagine I will develop some idiosyncrasies of my own,' Hull said, observing the ragman, who had paused at a nearby table to upend the remains from several tumblers into his mouth before carrying them one-handed, a finger dipped into each, through a door near the counter. It led outside to a wood-screened kitchen of sorts where two coloured women took it in turns to clean the drinking vessels in a tub of cold, grey water. Curses could be heard coming through the still-open door. The tumblers had been emptied of their dregs and the women knew by whom.

Fox ignored the commotion and replied, 'No doubt about that. No doubt at all. Mr Tweed used to dress the coloured constables in old red coats and garlands and march them up and down the main street from time to time. Missed the army, I expect.'

'Well,' said Hull trying to reconcile this with the man he had met at Port Nolloth. 'Well,' he said again, and changed the subject. 'How did it happen that you came to be here, Dr Fox?'

'It is not much of a story, I'm afraid. When I was about your age I went over to Paraguay as the company doctor of a British textile factory. Things became frightening under Lopez's rule – hundreds of people killed daily out of sheer paranoia. Even his own family was not safe, you know. As a foreigner, I was at risk too and it took terribly long for us British to be allowed out of the country. I fled to the Cape and eventually ended up here.'

'And you are happy here?'

'Oh yes. I treat a few fevers and coughs, try to teach the natives about hygiene as best I can. That sort of thing, you know. Now,' he said, standing up, 'I will be wanted back at Okiep, but I'll see you there on Saturday. The Super is having a small reception at his home and you've been invited. Dress is formal, and make sure to wear your dancing shoes. So long for now, old fellow.'

After Fox left, the native with the rag stood at the table

wiping it down, unconcerned by Hull's presence. The beer in his hand was heavy. He took one more sip and placed it on the table. As he rose, the native took the near-full mug and brought it to his mouth, drinking it down in three gulps.

Noki continued walking in the heat of the winter's day. Before him now lay an ascent through tumbled boulders and ashen scrub. Between these he found dassie middens, and he stooped for the darkest turds to place in his mouth for moisture. At least a day had passed since he had had sufficient water. Earlier that morning he had dug a hole that yielded a tablespoonful, live with animalcules and grains of sand that he encountered long afterwards in his teeth. As the incline progressed, the sinking tread on the flat sand ceased, making way for the monotony of hauling body from rock to rock. Noki knew what awaited him atop the koppie. A mockery of distance in which hill followed hill. Each the same, comprised of scattered rocks and bare shoulders of smooth stone. Stone too smooth for his hand to claw hold of, that shredded his trousers seat with each descent. For hours these aching rises had made up his view. Each summit an insult with its rolling koppies echoing one another, so that those preceding became only a dream of those to follow.

Blinking in the sharp late-afternoon light, shielding his eyes with his hand, he saw at last the valley containing Springbokfontein; the cluster of buildings, and then on the rises, near the mine, the shelters of the native labourers. He began his descent in dull twilight, hearing the sound of machines and voices calling, smelled the smokestack. His feet sank in the sand, and he prepared his nose as he reached the outskirts of the settlements. The air was fouled with the carcasses of buck and goats, rotting vegetable peelings, faeces and urine that formed a pooling soup on the sandy ground. There were tins and broken barrels amongst it, worn-out bridles and rusting tools, porcupine quills, a ladder with splintered rungs, a flowered teacup with a torn lip, a partly burnt woollen blanket.

In the distance, he could see naked children scavenging, while nearby a pack of jackals pulled at the carcass of a sheep, its face grinning, stomach spilling yellow as the scrub it had eaten. Noki ducked, lifted a can and threw it at them, testing the dryness of his voice by croaking what had been meant as a shout. The jackals looked up, sniffed the air, but scenting no danger from him, returned to feeding. He stepped carefully now, barefoot through the rubble. In the dull light he kicked a bottle, hearing it roll and clink as it met another.

He had reached the children. They were from the Bushman camp at the outskirts of the settlement, and cowered over their treasures at the sight of him – a rancid hock of goat meat, knotted ends of wire, a piece of material that may have once belonged to a woman's skirt. They had been instructed in fear, these children from a tribe of small dusty-skinned people who every few months came out of the desert and sought money. Somewhere they had learnt the habit of alcohol, and it drove them ever back to the mines where they walked miles each day collecting firewood to sell to the Company. When they had made enough money, they drank for days before returning to the desert and the quiet, hard life that awaited them there.

They were viewed as uncivilised, monkeyed creatures who communicated by means of clicks and hand signals. In certain areas they were hunted for sport by white men, families of them recorded on tintypes as a memento to mark a successful day's shooting. Many of them carried dreadful scars on their backs from whippings meted out when some 60 of them had been rounded up as pests and sent by ship to Cape Town to be worked as servants. But they could not be untrained of their savagery; unable to use tools, ignorant of vegetable gardens, of field work, of scrubbing kitchen floors or liverying horses. Their masters wearied of thrashing them, and soon the Bushmen vanished from the Cape, drifting back by whatever means towards the desert. Many others, not only natives, were scarred by the whip, but on the Bushmen, these small creatures barely larger than children, it seemed most cruel.

Noki continued on towards the settlement, passing the slight shacks of the Bushmen, then the Zulu huts and the round matjies houses of the Nama, all the while being watched by dark faces lit by campfires. Babies cried, pots of pap cooked on open fires. Men smoked pipes of tobacco diluted with dry leaves and twigs. Coughing and spitting sounded all around, accompanied by the low hum of a tune being sung somewhere. Women, hardly more than girls, hunched near fires, some of them murmuring invitations to him for a few minutes of paid fumblings on a stinking goat hide. There were times when loneliness had driven Noki to seek company in this way, but tonight he ignored them. He was tired and hungry, wanting to be home.

Even so, he took the time to pause at the hut of a friend of his named Tengo. The two of them and another man, Moses, worked together on an underground team captained by a Cornishman, Jory Tregowning. It was common then to refer to all Cornishmen as Cousin Jacks, both fondly and as an insult, but the three men reserved the term for their captain alone. He was a good man and they admired him. He worked hard, made them work hard too, yet he took the time to teach them more skills and knowledge than they would otherwise have had. In short, he was as close to an ally on the mines as any native might expect in a white man.

'I've returned, my friend,' Noki said as he pushed aside the goatskin that covered the entrance to Tengo's hut.

'Welcome back,' Tengo replied, inviting Noki to come in and sit on a reed mat and gulp from a clay pot of beer. 'I hope you're not too tired from your journey. The Cousin Jack said we begin sinking the new shaft when you return. Your mine has been waiting for you.'

'You haven't begun it yet? Anele was a poor substitute then,' he laughed. 'My little brother isn't as strong as me.'

Tengo shook his head. 'No, I have to tell you something that you won't want to hear. Anele's been wild while you were away. You know how he's always trying to show that he's a man, and so he fell in with some men who smuggled a cask of Cape Smoke up from the Port. He drank with them, got drunk. They took all his money, to pay for the liquor, they said, but it was thievery, plain and simple. And so he became violent, trying to take it back from them. He beat one of them. It was bad, a bad fight. Cloete had to arrest him.'

Noki put the clay pot on the ground. 'How long ago?' But when Tengo didn't answer quickly enough he shouted, 'How long? How many days has he been in jail?'

'Maybe two weeks now.'

'These men – the ones that took his money – who are they? Which men?'

'Basters.'

They were known by several names, but it was Baster that was most common, as they were a tribe descended from the bastard children of Dutch men and native women. In the Dutch colonies they had been trained for war, put into lightly armed commandos that fought on horseback, killing Bushmen and Hottentots that gave trouble. But eventually they tired of their mercenary life and set off under the rule of a Kaptijn to make a home for themselves elsewhere. The clan that could be found at Springbokfontein had split from the rest of the tribe, taking the land from the Nama Hottentots, naming it their own through violence. Prone to ferocity, and with a sense of pride that came from being part-white, the Basters were unpopular on the mines. They spoke of the land being theirs, of it being owed to them by their fathers and promised to them by God. They were angry too, hating their fathers who had not wanted them and hating their mothers for being black. They spoke Dutch and English as well as any white man, wore clothes as well made as theirs, yet they were not considered good enough. Still, on the mines they were treated better, paid more, had some rights that the savage tribes did not share.

Noki stalked across the strip of fastidiously maintained no man's land that separated the Baster settlement from the others. There were no rotting carcasses here, nor the leavings from ablutions. The small colony was referred to as the Baster Village or simply the Village, signalling it as something distinct from all that it neighboured. The Village was guarded by sentries at regular intervals so that they seemed to inhabit the role of posts in an unwired fence. Noki approached one, who looked at him from his half-slouch, his lip curled in disapproval. He spoke in broken Dutch, requesting to see their leader, Adam Waterboer. The sentry was reluctant, moving from one arm to the other a rifle of such ancient make that it could not possibly have fired. He looked again at the native before him, turned his head and called something to another sentry a hundred yards away. Then the ancient rifle was lowered and a head cocked with the command to follow.

Noki tailed the sentry through a labyrinth of streets that ran with water. Women had been washing the clothes their husbands had worn underground that week. Shirts hung dripping on ropes strung between the dwellings. Only the Basters could afford to own more than one outfit of clothing and had water enough to waste on washing.

He was led inside a canvas tent. A lamp burned on a wooden table at which a man he knew to be Waterboer sat reading a Dutch Bible. He wore a suit and cravat and a clean white shirt with a stiff collar. His hair was down to his shoulders, brushed back to show the length of it, that it did not curl. After several moments of mute concentration, he looked up at Noki with mud-green eyes. 'The blessings of God be upon you,' he greeted the native, but did not invite him to sit down. 'You have asked to see me and so you have been brought forward, as the blind and cripple were brought to our Lord. What is the malady that has made you come to me with such urgency, neighbour?'

'My name is Molefi Noki. I have come about my brother, Anele Noki. He is a sorter at the Blue Mine, but was working underground while I was away harvesting my crop.'

Waterboer nodded and stroked his hair with the palm of his hand. 'I know the one. He wears a faded red shirt that has been patched at the shoulder.'

'Yes, that is my brother.'

'And what is your brother to me that you have come before me without even taking the time to wash the dust from your face?'

Noki fisted his hands at his sides. 'Some of your men got him drunk. They took his money and he tried to get it back from them. He was arrested for that.'

'Liquor is a curse,' the Griqua chief sighed as he elbowed the table with both arms and joined his hands under his chin. 'It is the liquid of Satan. My men know this. They know that a drop of that poison will see them in the fires of hell. God will punish them.'

'I have no interest in your God punishing them. It is you that needs to punish them for what they have done to my brother.'

'Tell me this: how old is your brother?'

'Seventeen.'

'Old enough to know better... had he been taught well.'

'You're wrong. My brother has been taught well, but your men took advantage—'

'My men? Did they force him to drink? Did they put Satan in his heart where God was never allowed? In fact, it was your brother who beat one of my men, your brother who tried to corrupt them with his untamed, evil ways. No, the truth is that you cannot point your finger here.'

'I'm telling you, he was arrested—'

'And he will be released soon enough.'

Noki bit his lip, spoke low. 'We are nothing in your eyes. To you we are nothing.'

'God loves us all equally and punishes us all equally. Your brother has sinned and now he is being punished. You cannot lay the blame for evil at the door of another man.'

Waterboer waved a hand in dismissal and returned to reading the large Bible. A moth flew around the lamp, crazed by the light, its wings softly brushing the grey strands at the man's shoulder. The sentry took Noki's arm and walked him out of the camp.

On Saturday afternoon Hull was washed and changed in preparation for his journey to Okiep. Genricks had packed an overnight bag for the magistrate, explaining, 'It'll be too late to be coming home afterwards, but you'll be staying in the hotel as the Super's guest.'

Hull had not ventured into town again since his drink with Fox. Through the late hours of each night, he could hear scuffles and laughter of drunks in the street. He preferred to stay within the space marked out for him by the neatly raked lines of Genricks, for the jailer brought him all he needed and saw to every aspect of his life. Should he turn to his left, Genricks would be ready at his elbow. Turning to the right, the same. Always the man was there, his shoulders hunched, his limp echoing unevenly on the wooden floors. From time to time he brought the magistrate small offerings in exchange for praise. A marbled pebble, as smooth and round as though it had been rolled by the sea; a black feather from a Verreaux's eagle, the length of a man's arm measured fingertip to shoulder; and small creatures that the jailer had carved out of wood – a horse, a tortoise, a korhaan and, last of all, the tenderly whittled head of a gemsbok, its long horns slightly crooked and sharp as needles.

It was Genricks who bathed Hull. He warmed potjies of water and carried them through to fill the metal bathtub without a grunt or strain. Then he assisted the magistrate in removing his bathrobe and folded it carefully on the seat of a kitchen chair that he had drawn nearby. A rag in his hand smoothed soap over Hull's body, commencing at the neck and shoulders, caressing his back with care. He stopped at the cleft of the buttocks, but moved to other places of intimacy such as armpits, backs of knees, between toes, behind ears. Afterwards he gave his hands to support Hull's climb from the tub and towelled him dry in the same pattern, before combing his hair and smoothing flyaways with dampened fingers. He dipped into the inner pocket of his worn corduroy jacket for a small pair of silver scissors

59

that might have been better suited to a lady's sewing basket, their blades engraved with flowers, the handles filigreed. These he used to snip at the magistrate's moustache and beard, following the line of his mouth with as much care as a lover might take, brushing away the cuttings with a soft hand and a light puff from his lips.

At 2pm the driver sent by Townsend arrived. Genricks stood with his hand raised in farewell, following the progress of the horse and cart until they had gone from view.

The day had been a cold one, yet the journey on the dirt track seemed to catch the sun at the right time. It warmed Hull, who had cooled somewhat since his bath. He was tired, and the steady motion of the cart lulled him to sleep, his chin tapping his collar. By now he had settled into a routine of sorts. He woke each day at 7, breakfasted at 8. At 9 he donned his robes and took up his position in the small courtroom in order to hear the cases brought before him. Sentences were passed and all duties completed by no later than midday, for there were few that warranted more than a quarter of an hour's attention. There was little that was taxing in the suits that came before him. They read as one crime repeated in various locations: drunks who had fought in the pub; drunks who had fought in the street; drunks who had fought in the settlements.

They were mostly men, native or Baster, but there were a few whites amongst them. That morning he had seen an Irishman accused of beating his common-law wife, a woman of Herero extraction. She had come to the mine one afternoon to ask the man for money, whispering to him as she drew him aside that their children were starving while he spent all his earnings in the pub. He had denied her request without words, answering instead with a fist to her jaw. Before the magistrate, the woman carried a thin, screaming baby. Four children with swollen bellies and stick limbs stood at her side. She declared that her milk had dried up, that they had not eaten in days.

Hull looked down at the prisoner, whose black hair resembled that of a person cartooned, the individual strands raised in fright. Yet the man was not afraid. Instead he was sullen, scowling at the room as two flaps of material gaped where his shirt had been torn. He had a large bruise on his right cheek, and a cut lip, which he licked regularly as though drawing attention to the harm done to him by the men who had pulled him from his wife.

'What do you have to say to the charges laid against you?' Hull asked.

'Nothin'.'

'Did you beat this woman?'

'I did.'

'Are these children yours?'

'Some of 'em maybe.'

'But you feel no responsibility towards them?'

The man did not reply, glared darkly at the thumbs of his bound hands.

'Jakob,' Hull turned his head towards the Baster assigned as his clerk, 'how many days has this man been locked up?'

'Two, sir.'

'Give him one more then, and may he have learnt his lesson by the end of that time.'

'Yes, sir.'

'Thank you, Constable Cloete, you can take him away. Next.'

Between cases Hull sipped water, blew his nose. The stench of the natives and drunks caused his head to ache, his eyes to water. Flies buzzed around the room. He gave orders to an old Nama man known as Oupa to pull harder on the rope that moved a horizontal contraption up and down, creating some breeze, dispersing the flies for a while.

At morning's end, Hull would leave the Magistracy through the door that opened into the passage of his residence. He would go to the bedroom, wash his face and hands, and by 12:30 was seated in the small-windowed dining room. He would hear the gruff humming of Genricks in the kitchen, smell his preparations of stew or roast or whatever had been found to cook for the meal that day. Hull made no requests with regard to the menu, knowing variety was not easily come by in this wilderness, though he rapidly tired of preserved fruit served with yellow cream for dessert. He prevaricated by attending to a scar on his finger, or by circling the bowl with a spoon. He ate corners of the fruit, small puffs of cream, allowing the rest to be marked by the spoon edge, but leaving it unconsumed.

Hull woke to the jolt of a wheel rolling free, a donkey's baulking cry. 'No,' he said, dreaming himself elsewhere, until the driver's hand was on him, hot breath in his face. 'Sorry, baas, sorry. You need to get out now, get out for some little minutes.'

He then remembered his journey to Okiep and, looking up, saw the nearness of the earth on the angled right side of the cart. He scrabbled down, asking, 'Are you able to fix the problem?'

'Oh yes, baas.'

'We will be late, you know,' he said, confirming the hour on his pocket watch.

'No, baas. It will be time. This happens always. A little minutes and we go again.'

Hull walked along the track a way. They had stopped on a slight incline and he was able to survey the surrounding landscape. He had already come to realise that he had been mistaken in his imaginings prior to arrival in Namaqualand. Here, too, was evidence of his error. Winter rains had brought a hue of green to the valley and surrounding hills. They had awoken the sand, so that now, as in his short ramblings near the cottage, he found flora that he considered miraculous: small pebble-like succulents blooming pink after the rain; strange trees with papery bark that shone silver in the midday heat and stood the height of a man; a shrub comprised of little more than two large leaves flat on the ground. And amongst all of this life a host of insects vibrated: lepidoptera, coleoptera, hymenoptera. There were bigger creatures too, he knew, for he found their droppings. Some he had seen. An ostrich in the distance, a tortoise asleep under a bush, meerkats that ducked and scattered at his approach.

Already within those few days since his arrival, he had begun to collect and catalogue the new world. Each day, after lunch, Hull exchanged his robes for a cream-coloured suit, his sensible shoes of the court for sturdy boots that supported his ankles in soft sand. He went into the wilderness that stretched out from behind the Residency into the hills beyond, accompanied by Oupa and the court translator, Ned. Young and strong, Ned carried an immense portfolio comprised of many double sheets of brown paper between which plant specimens were pressed. The old man carried a wide-mouthed jar of poisonous liquid.

Both assistants approximated the dress of civilised men. Ned wore a shirt, trousers, jacket, and shoes over sockless feet. Oupa went barefoot in a pair of trousers so large that the bottoms were doubled three times over, the weight of them causing the folds to buckle and dip. His shirt was equally large, tucked into a rope that belted the man's thin waist, the shirt-back billowing comically on his small frame. He tugged at the neck, the armpits, pulling the cloth away from his skin with discomfort. The old man was knowledgeable, holding within him a lifetime of observation that allowed him to point unerringly at spots to dig for fat yellow scorpions or the burrows of sand moles and other creatures. He could recognise footprints in the scattered grains of soft sand or discover a lair simply by following a stray thread of fur on a leaf. He cocked his head to the side and overheard the conversation of insects, was able to distinguish the voices of one from another.

Ned, when asked by the magistrate about his name, said simply that it had been given him by a mine boss when he was a young boy helping his mother sort ore. Later he had served as messenger for the same man, running errands underground, above ground, in the settlements, sometimes stretching his legs all the way to Okiep or Nababeep and back. In this way the boy had become exposed to the variety of people, foreigners and natives, that made up the copper mining workforce. Ned changed his voice or accent slightly according to whom he was translating for, and his features altered too, so that he uncannily aged half a century when speaking on behalf of Oupa. He embodied the woe or fear, the violence or arrogance of those in the dock, his voice matching their expressions, their stances, their behaviour. Though Hull was not certain, he felt that he recognised something unflattering and high-pitched in Ned's voice whenever he translated the magistrate's words, his chin visibly weakening as he spoke.

From time to time as the three men walked, Oupa paused to indicate where to dig for tubers and insects. He chewed on the leaves of certain plants, veered away from others. On a rock, he identified an armoured lizard that played dead at his touch. When Hull went to investigate, the creature bit its tail, making a plated circle of defence. He lifted it and dropped it into the jar that Oupa carried, watching as the lizard gaped its tail free, clawed the liquid, unable to catch hold of the glass sides. Death was swift, and before long it was still, mouth and eyes open, legs spread out in frenzy as ants and beetles floated around it. When Oupa complained, Hull explained, 'I am studying your animals. I want the world to know about your beautiful creatures. This is the only way to do it.'

Oupa made a response, but Ned did not translate and Hull did not insist. Yet, after that incident the old man no longer pointed out any living thing to the magistrate. He followed, dutiful as a servant, keeping his eyes downward, carrying the jar as uncomfortably as he wore his clothes.

After dismissing his assistants for the evening, Hull went through to the second bedroom, which he used as a study. Here he carefully sieved his findings from the jar, cleaning and drying them with care. He pinned them in rows on corkboard, or stored them in cottonwool-lined boxes. Reptiles and rodents were transferred to individual jars of formaldehyde and stored on shelves that the sun did not reach. Plant specimens were placed between fresh sheets of brown paper, inter-spliced with drying sheets that, infant-like, required regular changing.

Each specimen, plant or animal, was labelled and recorded in a logbook, keeping track of date, time of day, weather conditions, size of specimen, sex, location and anecdotal stories that may have been supplied. For example, a specific locust, Oupa pointed out, if found chirping incessantly on the roof of a single hut, foretold that a relative had died. Catching the insect in order to silence it was to no purpose – the death had already occurred; its song had only brought news of the passing.

In this manner the nights went by, Hull talking to himself as he measured and examined, scratching his pen across the pages, trying to understand the dead things that surrounded him.

By the time he reached Okiep, the afternoon was coming to a close, yet still the town's mine heaps were alive with movement. The driver had stopped outside a large house with a fresh white fence and white-washed walls. It was lined with neatly kept hydrangeas growing in pots of black soil that must have been imported from elsewhere.

'Well, you're late!' the Super said, coming outside.

'Yes, I am afraid there was a small accident, but—'

'These damned roads. Damned blasted roads. Well, never mind all that now. Let's have some tea. Meet the family before you go to the hotel to freshen up and we'll say no more about it.'

'Thank you. A cup of tea would be very welcome.'

'Yes, yes. Come along.'

The Super led Hull through the front door into an enclosed hall where a native stood. 'Stay there,' he said, before passing through a further door. The native approached with a horsehair brush and began to sweep it across Hull's clothing and shoes, causing great clouds of dust to swell up around them. Hull sneezed, sneezed again, fumbling for his handkerchief. When he had done, the native opened the door, allowing the magistrate to proceed into a carpeted passageway where Townsend waited. 'That's more like it. Now, this way.'

They stepped into a heavily wallpapered sitting room in which two women were seated, and who looked up with smiles at Hull's entrance. The oldest of these, Mrs Townsend, had been embroidering bluebells on a piece of linen, but put it aside as her husband introduced her.

'Mr Hull,' she said, rising, 'we are so pleased to have you with us. We have been looking forward to your appointment for some time. But we do feel for you so very much. To be out here, away from everything you have known... It is too awful. You must consider this your home and come to visit us as often as you like. The ride is not so long, you know. Please, do sit down. Kitty, dear, ring for tea.' A young lady, who had been engaged in reading as he entered, put her book on the table and stood to ring the bell.

'These are my daughters, Mr Hull. Katrina,' she indicated. The bell ringer curtseyed and lowered her eyes as she smiled. 'And this is my youngest, Mrs McBride, whom you have already met, I believe.'

Hull turned. She was seated on a low stool beside the window, slightly shielded by a table with a large ornamental Chinese vase on it, which had resulted in his not observing her until then. She moved a little at the waist and greeted him, though she did not rise. It was the first time that he had seen her without her veil and he was surprised to find the marks of her past illness on her cheeks and forehead, visible and livid from across the room. They unsettled him and he looked away hurriedly, even as he returned her greeting.

Katrina offered him a seat in a wingback chair and he blushed, sitting down awkwardly. 'Thank you,' he said, then 'thank you' again, this time to Mrs Townsend. 'I am very pleased to be here. It is kind of you to invite me. I am very pleased. You are most kind.'

An aproned servant entered the room with a tray of tea and biscuits.

'Please forgive us for these biscuits, Mr Hull. We were let down by the supply ship. We wanted to make jam tarts, but the fruit did not come,' Katrina said.

'I am sure—'

'Yes, we were bitterly disappointed. We did not know what to do. Poor Kitty cried terribly.'

'Please do not be concerned on my behalf. You are very kind. I am pleased to be here. I am quite happy simply to be in company.'

'I told them a biscuit is as good as a cream cake to a bachelor,' said the Super. 'But what does a father know about delicacies and niceties and such? To them I am an oaf, isn't that right, my dears?'

'But poor Mr Hull,' Mrs Townsend said.

69

'Yes, poor Mr Hull. Are you very lonesome?' said Katrina. She raised her eyes to the magistrate's as she asked her question, but lowered them again hastily in a manner that seemed rehearsed. 'We couldn't bear to hear that.'

'Well, not lonesome as such—'

'I know what will cheer you up!' said Katrina, leaving the room and returning a moment later with an enormous long-haired angora cat, its limbs slack in her arms. 'This is our lovely Hortense. She's the only cat in Namaqualand. There's a breeder in Durban and she came all the way to us here in a basket with a guard to keep her from being stolen.' She placed the cat on Hull's knees where it dug its claws into his thighs and then leapt off, walking stiffly.

'Oh, yes, very charming. But actually, you know, I have seen another cat,' he said. 'At the hotel in Port Nolloth.'

'No, that is not possible! Hortense is the only cat. Tell him, Papa.'

'You're mistaken, Hull.'

Hull looked at the carpet. 'Well, yes, I suppose I am. I must be.'

'We love her so much, silly Hortense,' Kitty continued. 'We have to take such care of her. She's always trying to get outside, but we keep her from it. Once the cookboy let her escape. It was terrible. Everyone had to stop work and then we found her on the roof. Poor thing, so frightened. Papa had to let the cookboy go after that.'

'I see,' said Hull, eyeing the cat where it perched on the windowsill beside Mrs McBride. 'But perhaps it would not be so very bad to allow her a few minutes outside each day, supervised of course. Only in your garden.'

'No, that would never do! She would get ever so dirty. And the natives would certainly catch her and eat her. They are very brutal, you know. Surely you wouldn't want us heartbroken, Mr Hull.'

'Why no, I only—'

Katrina lowered her eyelids. 'Surely you want only

good things for us.'

Hull glanced about the room. He could think of no suitable response. At the window, Mrs McBride had turned away from the conversation, her cup and saucer clattering too loudly as she placed them on the table beside the vase. She shook her head a little, dipped it as her sister spoke. Hull smiled at his hostesses, reached across for one of the biscuits. In his mouth it was as dry as the dust that had been brushed from him.

At dinner he was placed between the two daughters. Mrs McBride remained in mourning black and went without ornament, while Katrina had covered herself in lace and jewels, her hair piled high upon her head in a variety of plaits and ringlets. She drew Hull's attention to the fact that the pheasants they were eating had been sent on the *Namaqua* in wooden cages. The birds had been fed until they could no longer fly, lifeless as tortoises they had become, she said. Did he find the flesh succulent? What were they dining on in the fine homes of the capital? This must surely be dull fare in comparison. Then, did he care for another helping of fresh peas, or gravy, perhaps a sharper knife? A cushion behind his back? She went on to instruct the servant to refill the magistrate's glass so regularly that he began to feel stifled and warmer than was comfortable.

He turned to the rest of the company. There were Dr Fox and a Mr Kitto, the Cornish mine boss from Okiep; a Reverend Brown, from the Anglican church, and his plump wife with a neck speckled with small brown moles; Mr Lyell, who organised the company's sporting events and who walked with the support of a cane; Mrs Lyell, who said little, her hands always near her husband, cutting his meat, assisting his shaking hands, offering him a spoon when the knife and fork he attempted to master proved too challenging. This small and shivering man had been a great wrestler in his day, but illness had crippled him, ageing him until he was reduced to a second childhood. Lastly there were Mr and Mrs Lincoln who ran the local store. Hull was not able to catch anyone's eye and did not like to call across the table, so that when Katrina began to say once more that she hoped he would visit them very often, he turned abruptly to her sister beside him. 'Mrs McBride, if I may, you're named for a flower and yet there are so few here.'

For a while she made no reply, twisting her fork in the pheasant on her plate. He noticed that even her earlobes and neck were pockmarked and he wondered whether the scars gave her any pain, whether talking or movement jarred them. He was about to turn away again, when she said, 'That is true at the moment, but in the springtime the flowers come out in such numbers and colours that it seems selfish to want them the rest of the year. I lived for a while with my husband in the great plains of California and in the deserts of Australia too. There they had nothing, no world at all aside from the rocks, or so it seemed to me, and I sometimes forgot that such things as flowers existed elsewhere. In that regard it is a relief to be here again, if only for the promise of flowers to come.'

'Indeed, I look forward to seeing that remarkable exhibition. I am very interested in flora and fauna, and all the components of our natural world.'

'There are few people of interest out here, Mr Hull, but in nature there is much to occupy you if you are patient enough to look for it.'

'Quite true. Already I have been surveying the area around my little cottage, but I fear it is too corrupted by the town. I would like to explore further afield. Perhaps even learn to hunt for larger game.'

Iris had kept her head lowered as they spoke. She continued to twist her fork, conversation seeming to come from her with some reluctance. Now she raised her eyes a little. 'We have a large thorn tree near the house. Birds sit in it, and they sing. I spent many years of my life watching them from the window or lying beneath its branches. I find that I do so again now that I have returned. There is some comfort in the repetition of such a familiar pastime.'

'It sounds very pleasant.'

'It can be, yes.'

'And are there other familiar pastimes that you have taken up again?'

'No. But the annual event, one in which I hope to be able to include my son this year, is the Company picnic. My father organises a trip out into the mountains or plains for all the miners and their families, and we are able to see so much more than is possible here in town.'

Hull smiled. 'A picnic? How very idyllic. I hope I shall be included in the party. I would greatly like to extend the range of my little expeditions. Indeed, I intend to do so very soon. However, I would need a white guide. My Hottentot assistants are not up to much and one of them in particular is becoming quite unhelpful.'

'Did I hear you say you need a guide?' asked Fox, causing all the guests to turn in Hull's direction.

'Well, yes, of sorts,' he said, embarrassed by the attention and lowering his voice a little. 'Someone who knows the area and who can also instruct me in hunting.'

'Ah, then Tregowning's your man. He goes out hunting and riding every weekend.'

'Tregowning!' said the Super from the head of the table. 'He's a troublemaker, that one. Needs to be watched. If he weren't such a damned good miner he would be out.'

'That's all very well,' Fox said, 'but I am sure we can agree that he knows the area better than anyone, and as a hunter you won't find a better man. I will have a word with him, Hull, when next I see him. Will that do?'

'Yes, thank you. You're very kind.'

'Well, Fox, just you make sure he behaves himself. I don't want him doing harm to my magistrate. They're damned difficult to come by, you know. Let it be on your head, do you hear?'

'Yes, Super. I can hear you very well. No one will harm Mr Hull, I assure you. He is quite safe.'

Later, in the drawing room, Hull sat, palms on knees, listening as Katrina played and sang. Then Mrs Townsend took over at the little upright pianoforte and the Super commanded: 'Dance!' The guests split into partners, shuffling miserably, shoulders curled inwards. Each felt the responsibility of politeness, and so they smiled at one another grimly, attempting jokes about the geography or the distance from the Cape. They drank more than might normally be considered good manners, but it assisted them in the making of pleasantries as the Super stalked the room, glaring at each couple.

Hull danced first with Katrina, before offering his arm to each of the married women in turn. Mrs Lincoln sweated into his hands and entertained him with a story about a horse that her husband had had to shoot in the week. Hull had heard the tale earlier in the evening and allowed himself to feign interest as he watched the Super advance on Mr Lyell, who was seated on a sofa, his hands and head shaking. Fingers were pointed, Townsend's face a riot of anger, until the old man hobbled to his feet and approached Katrina where she leaned crossly beside a corner table. She shook her head at the old man's request, but stood up with Kitto when he stepped forward a moment later under her father's instructions.

Some time afterwards, his feet heavy and cheeks stiff, Hull was able to escape into the hallway. He gave a sigh and rested his back against the papered wall, wondering when the night might at last be over.

'You are tired,' came a voice, and he looked up to find that at the farther end of the hallway, deep in the shadows, stood Mrs McBride. She was holding up a lace curtain and looking out into the darkness, but she let it drop now as Hull turned to her, saying, 'Yes, I am afraid I am. I am not much accustomed to dancing.'

'My father does not easily tire of watching his guests enjoying themselves. Even if their enjoyment has long since ceased.'

He laughed a little. 'And are you enjoying yourself?'

'Most of these people I have seen every day since my return. I enjoy them as much tonight as at any other time.'

Hull was uncertain what to say, mumbling, 'Well, yes, I imagine it can be...'

Seeing his confusion, Mrs McBride stepped forward. 'Forgive me, Mr Hull, I have a headache. I believe I will return to the drawing room and sit down.'

'Of course.'

She walked past him, pausing as she reached the door. 'I wonder whether perhaps it is not better to grow accustomed to a place such as this early on. I could never accept it and I left at the first opportunity. Now that I find myself here again, it seems to me that a person should be resilient in order to remain.'

'Well, yes. Well, certainly. Resilience, yes.'

She opened the door and returned to the drawing room, the notes of a tune being sung poorly falling dully into the hallway.

Well after midnight Dr Fox and Hull walked together towards the hotel. It was bitterly cold and Hull shoved his hands deep into his trouser pockets. His face and back had been drenched in sweat from the enforced dancing, and now, out in the open, that moisture was like a band of steel around him. It seemed to squeeze his innards, causing his nose and eyes to run, a wet cough to force itself up from his lungs. All else was quiet in the town, each window dark, the inhabitants asleep.

Fox filled and lit a pipe, sighing, 'Thank God that is done. These dinners are damned tedious, but we must attend.'

'Mrs Townsend is very kind,' Hull said.

'But the daughters are odious. Absolutely dreadful.'

'The younger one – Mrs McBride – has been unwell, I believe?'

'Oh, you mean the scarring? Yes, a shame that. I've given her oils for the marks, but God knows if she uses them. They don't seem to be getting any better. Pity. She's not too ugly under all those blemishes, even if she is a strange girl. She never could settle down here, you know, was always running off into the wilderness, always shouting and making scenes. A very unpleasant girl in her time, you know.'

'I find that hard to believe.'

'Well, it's true, on my honour. But she appears to have been tamed these past years. No doubt by circumstances.'

'Which circumstances are those?'

'She was always such a wild, foolish girl, and the first man who came along, well, she married him, no matter that he was an ancient, hideous old soak. Some mining investor or other; that's what he called himself anyway. He came out here to inspect the mines, see if it was worth putting his money into them, but decided against it. When he left, she went off with him.'

'You don't mean to tell me that it was an elopement?'

'More or less. It certainly was no kidnapping.'

77

They walked in silence a few paces. Hull looked towards the darkness of the mine, watched the motion of the beam pump. It was still thrusting, its black pistons and cogs directing a great arm that reached down into the earth with a cupped hand to quench its endless thirst.

'They were happy at least?' he said at last.

'Who's that? Oh, you mean Mrs McBride, eh? I couldn't say. But it seems unlikely from what I've heard. There was some money at first, you know, but by the time of his death he was a bankrupt, fleeing creditors in Australia, and already living in debt in the most atrocious lodgings, just off the docks in Cape Town. Left her nothing when he died, you know. Not a penny. Nothing for herself or the boy, nothing to secure their futures.'

'That is sad indeed.'

'Well, she won't be the first impoverished young widow, nor the last. Though her chances of marrying again are slim now. Not out here, and not with those deformities.'

'I suppose so, yes.'

'But never mind Mrs McBride, it's Kitty that you need to be thinking about.'

'How so?'

'How so?' laughed Fox. 'Really Hull, you are quite naïve. She's set her cap at you, haven't you noticed?'

The magistrate coughed. 'Surely not! Though she did talk a vast amount. Her cat—'

'Yes, she's a clever girl, for all her faults. She knows that she needs a husband and she knows what she is supposed to do in order to get one. Plays coy and innocent, but she will have her claws in you faster than you can say "Hortense",' he laughed.

Hull reached into his breast pocket for a handkerchief and blew his nose.

'Never mind, my man. You needn't be caught if you don't wish to be. Tell me, how is work coming along?'

He was happy to change the subject and said, 'I believe it is going well. But perhaps you can help me to understand a case I have been dealing with. A farmer came in asserting that some mining men had killed three of his sheep. They were caught in the act by the farmer himself and he said he had witnesses to confirm his version of events. However, when the witnesses were called, they denied having seen any such thing. They said the farmer had killed the sheep himself. The farmer became irate. I had to have him removed from the room. His name is Van den Bosch. Do you know him? Is he unreliable?'

'Not unreliable, no.' Fox looked around as though there might be someone listening in all that darkness, then lowered his voice as he continued, 'But you would be wise to be careful in dealings with him. See to it that the case is dismissed.'

Hull sniffed, blew his nose again. 'I have no choice but to dismiss it, what with the witness testimonies.'

'Van den Bosch angered the Super. Something about grazing land. He's boycotted now. The CCMC does not do business with him any longer.'

'What does that have to do with the case?'

'No doubt the witnesses have been paid off or threatened so that the miners responsible for killing the sheep can be protected.'

'But they are under oath!'

'Come now, Hull, let's leave it at that. It's Company business. Best left alone, eh? Keep our noses out of what doesn't concern us, that's for the best.' He paused outside a cottage. 'Well, here we are. My little home. Will you come in for a whiskey?'

'No. No, thank you.'

'Yes, better not, it's late enough as it is and I have cases to attend to tomorrow. No day of rest for me, you know. Now, will you find your way back to the hotel? It's just two buildings up on your right.'

'Yes, I will manage. Thank you, Dr Fox, I appreciate all your advice. I am – well – I am not always certain, you see. It is very different here. The law, I mean. The way

79

things work. I am glad to have found a friend in you to guide me.'

'Of course, my man, of course. What are we here for if not to help our neighbours? You ask me on any matter, at any time. I will always assist you if I can. It was good to see you tonight, and I'll pop by some time in the week for a visit. Remember to dismiss that case, won't you?'

'Yes, I will.'

'Fine, fine. I'll say goodnight then.'

A fortnight had passed since Noki's return to the mines. Attempts to learn anything further about his brother's incarceration had failed. He had been denied access to the prison, and had been unable to speak to the jailer, who was never in his office now. Always Genricks was at the Residency, working at his chores, whistling through his teeth, or else standing on the stoep with his arms crossed, eyeing the town as though everything within it, the cottage included, belonged to him.

In the evening Noki went into the yard of the Residency, shadowing a tree known as the half-man, and watched the jailer's movements. He noted the limp, hunched shoulders, the way the man fingered his teeth after a meal to release fragments, rolling them on his tongue before swallowing. Genricks raked the sand, watered shrubs. Later, candlelight followed him as he carried a cup and saucer to the kitchen, as he pulled to the curtains in every room.

When the jailer left for the night, it was with hands full. A shirt that fish moths had been at, apples in his pockets, a book from which the cover had come loose and which he had said he would repair, and a greasy drumstick left over from the magistrate's dinner.

'Boss Genricks?' Noki said, stepping out from behind the tree.

The jailer looked at him, took a bite from the drumstick. 'What you want, kaffir?'

'Please, boss, it is only a question about my brother, Anele. I only want to know——'

'This ain't the time nor it ain't the place. Fuck off 'fore I arrest you.' He tossed the bone aside, walked on.

Constable Cloete was of no assistance either. He drank down the tumbler of brandy that Noki stood him at the bar, shrugging, 'The only time I even see the prisoners is when I bring them in and out of the jail. I took your brother into custody, handed him over, that was it. Sorry.'

Afterwards, Noki returned to the Residency's grounds, looked for movement in the room he knew to be the magistrate's study, lamplight dull through the curtains. He paused outside the window, his hands on the ledge, wondering what the man was doing inside, what it was that kept him up this late. He thought of going to the door, knocking. Thought of asking the magistrate directly about Anele. But he caught his reflection in the glass – the dark nothingness of his face, the startling light of his eyes inside it, so bright that he had taken them at first for patches of moonlight. He stared back at himself, blinked, and then the curtain was twitching, was being moved aside, and Noki ducked out of view.

'Is that you, Genricks?' came the magistrate's voice. 'Genricks?'

The curtain closed again, and behind it the light rippled as Hull raised a lamp and carried it from the room. A door closed. Another opened, closed. Only darkness was left now. Not even the reflection of Noki's eyes had remained to look back at him, to observe him where he stood.

On Saturdays they worked a half-day. Noki came up out of the earth, thick with filth, and stood in line to collect his wages. Afterwards he did not follow the others back to the settlement. Instead he left the town, walking the dirt of the mine out into the surrounding veld, hoping for signs indicating in which direction the prisoners had been taken to collect firewood. The horizon offered no clue, nor did the sand, empty as it was of footprints. He saw only in the distance the halting form of the magistrate, bending and rising, bending and rising as his servants followed.

The afternoon was darkening into nightfall when Noki began to retrace his steps homewards. Already he could hear voices, music. There was to be a birthday celebration at the pub that night for the postmaster's dog. Every couple of months it was given one as an excuse for a party, though little incentive was required on paydays for men to drink and gather.

He saw now ahead of him, treading heavily through the scrub, the 12-year-old son of his friend Moses. The boy was weighted down by something slung across his shoulders.

'Hey, Solomon. What have you got there?'

'I've been checking my snares. Got this duiker, and a couple of korhane.'

'Let me help you.'

'No, I can do it myself,' the boy said, standing taller under the carcass. 'But you can walk with me if you like. My father and some friends are at our hut.'

'They will not go to the party?'

'For a dog? What for when we've beer at home that will cost nothing to drink?'

Noki laughed. 'You're right.'

When they arrived at the hut, Moses rose from the upturned crate on which he had been seated. His arms were wide as he spoke. 'See, friends, my son has caught the meat that we'll eat tonight.'

Solomon toed the ground, covered his mouth as the

men cheered his success.

'You're becoming a man,' said Zamikhaya.

'What are you saying?' said Coffin John – a corruption of the white miners' nickname for him of Coughing John. 'This is not a boy any more. This is already a man. I can see it with my own eyes.'

'Not yet,' said Solomon. 'Only when I go underground like my father, like all of you, then I'll be a man.'

'Yes,' said Noki. 'That's the true moment of circumcision, when we are cut off from the daylight and thrown into darkness. That's when we truly leave behind our boyhood.'

'So, Noki, here you are,' said Moses, offering his guest a seat on a log beside the fire. 'Did you see Anele?'

'No. I couldn't find the prisoners. I don't know if they went out today. There was no sign of them that I could find.'

Coffin John passed him the bowl of beer. 'Have you tried with money?'

'I left all my savings for my wife when I went home. I've only got my wages and that is too little to bribe a man like Genricks.'

The men nodded.

'He does what he likes, that one. Even if you bribed him, he wouldn't help you,' said Zamikhaya.

'What about Waterboer, can he do anything?' said Moses.

'When I brought Anele to the mines it was Waterboer I had to bribe to get him a job. "We take care of each other, we are all God's children," was what he said. But when my brother is in jail, he has no interest at all. When we're poor and helpless then we're no longer God's children. Then we're animals left to die.'

'Those Basters cast us from our jobs when they want one for their brothers and uncles. But if we want a job for our brother then we have to go begging to Waterboer and put all our savings in his hand and hope he will talk to

84

Reid and that we won't starve. I fucking hate them,' said Zamikhaya.

Coffin John wheezed, patted his chest. 'With one hand he takes our money. The other is raised to the sky in praise of his god.'

'You know what they say about him?' said Zamikhaya. 'They say he goes out into the koppies and mates with the baboons. He pushes them up against the rocks and puts his tiny little cock in them until they howl and howl.'

'Owooohooo,' called Moses, and the men laughed, adding their own imitations, stamping their feet.

'That can be your bribe,' laughed Coffin John. 'Catch a baboon bride for old Waterboer, eh.' A rough bout of coughing racked the man's chest. He spat up something black and slimy onto the ground beside him.

Noki laughed into the beer, wiped his mouth. 'A good idea, Coffin. A good idea.'

The boy edged back towards them from behind the hut where he had been skinning the duiker. He laughed too, though he had not heard the joke, and sat a little way outside the circle of men, listening to their howls and crudities with an ear for later imitation. Noki passed the beer to him, smiled. He thought of his brother, felt that he recognised in Solomon the same desire for manhood, the same urge to be amongst men. Anele too had sat with them in this way, had eyed their work-thickened fingers, had held out his own for self-examination, priding himself on his callouses when they had come.

He recalled workday mornings past, waking in the dark, stumbling outside to coals still glowing from the previous night's fire. Blowing on them, adding twigs until there was enough of a blaze to boil a small amount of water, into which he threw coffee grounds. Most days he did not bother to reheat the pap from the night before, eating it stiff and cold with his fingers, though sometimes, if it had been left uncovered, insects would be glued to it and he had to scoop them out, flick them to the ground. By then the morning chorus of hacking coughs would have begun as other workers woke, each series of coughs punctuated by spitting. And all around the sounds of urine on wooden sides, of people stumbling off to defecate. Water splashing onto faces. Spoons ringing against cooking pots. From the Baster settlement the wailing of hymns sung too loudly. Everywhere children crying at being woken to go to work, women angry, shouts and threats. Many with no more for breakfast than the smell of woodsmoke and a quarter-cup of coffee begged off a neighbour.

Usually Noki allowed Anele to sleep until the very last moment, waking him with a touch on his shoulder, watching as his brother's eyes opened in surprise. Every day that expression of surprise as though it were the first day, as though the coming labour and the sea of rocks washing his way to be crushed and sorted, all of it, was unexpected. Perhaps when he returned from jail he would have altered. Perhaps he would no longer have the ability to be surprised. He would be as they all were. Broken down into acceptance.

Around the fire the laughter had stopped. Moses said, 'Have you heard? Wheal Burra is closing. They are letting people go.'

'Already?' said Coffin John.

'What will happen to the workers?' asked Noki.

Zamikhaya brought a fist down on his thigh. 'Are you even asking? They'll come here and starve or they'll go home and starve.'

'But if they're skilled men then the mine needs them. Too many have already left for the gold mines.'

'Yes, and the Company doesn't replace them because they see how nice it is not to spend money. So, if we lose, say, twenty men, they hire maybe ten.'

'Not even ten,' said Coffin John.

'That's what I'm saying. Not even ten.'

'For them it's only one word. For them it's all about profit.'

'Profit!' shouted Zamikhaya. 'When did we ever see this profit? We dig up the copper, but do we have any, here, in our hands? No, we don't even have a road that we didn't make with our own feet. We have nothing.'

'I understand you,' said Moses, 'but what can we do? We have to eat, don't we? We have to care for our families. That's all there is to it. What can come from complaining?'

The boy leaned forward. 'Maybe, do you think, maybe it is better at the new mines, up there on the Rand?'

'Not a chance,' said Zamikhaya, and 'Mining is mining,' replied Coffin John hoarsely. 'Where are the mines? Underground. How is the air? Full of dust. Where are our homes? Far away. Where is the money? In the pocket of the Company.'

Zamikhaya nodded and pointed at the boy. 'That's it. Exactly that. One day you'll know that for yourself. Here or there, it's all the same.'

A spark jumped free of the fire. It landed on the boy. For a second Solomon's shirt showed yellow, his chin and brow orange. He smothered the light with his hand. Even so, Noki could see his body glowing, his eyes aflame in the dark.

Hull woke at his desk, the journal in which he recorded his findings open before him. His head had rolled back, saliva lightening the hairs of his beard in the semi-darkness. The lamp guttered eerily across his bottled specimens so that they appeared to be in motion, their bodies squirming with life, snouts and claws rapping at the glass.

From the direction of the pub came the playing of mouth organs, singing and cheers. Hull rose stiffly and rubbed his neck. The clock on the mantel had long since chimed midnight. He neatened his desk, pushed in the chair and returned a cup to its saucer. It was time for bed, and yet, despite the night being cold, he was reluctant to go. There was too much noise outside, too much to be at ease. How could he sleep while that continued? He opened the window and peered out, thinking by the action to silence the revellers somehow. But the laughter continued, and he shut it again.

For a time he paced the room, the clamour having brought an unusual restlessness to his limbs. Soon, however, he drew to a halt. Already so large at his arrival, the furniture now seemed to have increased in size, indeed, seemed to be growing before him. He felt certain that at any minute the carpet would be swallowed up, himself with it. Everything was altered, monstrous. The pages of his books looked ghostly, transparent even, so that he stared straight through them at the swelling desk, while all around him the unearthly movement of preserved creatures persisted, crept towards him, came ever closer until he could feel their breath on him, their cold, wet breath. He drew up his arms against his face and hastened from the room, from the cottage itself.

Outside the night was tar dark. He made towards the light of the pub, breathing in cold gasps. A fiddle was being tuned. A dog howled. And, with no more warning than a snorting rush, an animal flung itself at Hull, knocking him to the ground. Claws scratched his face, the beast hissing and bellowing. He reached up to protect himself, but instead of fur or scales, he felt coarse cloth under his hand, and arms and legs. He pushed the person from him, stood up and struck a match to reveal a woman on her back, grunting, her long hair loosed about her. He held the match up to his face, allowing her a moment to see her mistake before the flame went out.

She clutched at sand. 'I'll kill him. I'll kill the bastard. I'll kill him.'

Hull rubbed his throat and passed a handkerchief over his smarting cheeks. 'Somebody has harmed you, madam?'

'Run off, he has! Gone to the gold mines, I know it! Left me to rot in this hole. Here!' she said, her voice heavy with drink as she held up something in the dark. 'Copper! Who ever heard of a copper wedding ring? It turns me finger green. Green!' She was insensible now, her fists sand-filled, her words ramshackle. 'Bastard copper, kill, copper kill. Green bastard.'

'I assure you, madam, no one has passed this way.' He lit another match and offered the woman his hand, helping her to her feet. 'No doubt he is at the festivities and you have missed him in the crowd.' She seemed smaller to him now as he shepherded her towards the pub; a tiny thing really. No threat at all. From time to time she whispered her strange words, but Hull hushed her, leading on.

Outside the pub, within the circle touched by the building's light, several men stood smoking pipes and drinking from unlabelled bottles. There was the sound of a conversation being swallowed at Hull's approach, then lips on bottlenecks and, 'Oh-ho, Jenny, what you caught there?'

'Shut your mouth,' she said.

The men laughed, and Hull said, 'Thank you gentlemen, that will do,' steering her towards the doorway. But he paused before entering, stopped by movement coming from the shadowy corner of the porch. Two figures were rutting unashamedly against the outer wall, doing nothing to temper their groans. Hull made to hurry into the building, but the woman had already turned and seen the coupling.

'I'll kill you, you're dead now, Mikey, dead!' she screamed, pulling the man off mid-thrust, and he stood surprised, failing to make himself decent. She fell on him, reaching for his eyes and ears, intent on ripping them out. He grabbed her wrists and held them at her sides, yet still she lashed out, stamping on his boots with her bare feet, spitting in his face.

In the meantime, a girl stepped out of the corner, adjusting her sackcloth dress. Hull saw with dismay her short woolly hair, her dark skin and eyes, the black of her nipples. He was discomfited by the way she sidled up to the jeering pipe-smokers, allowing several to share her in a half-spirited grope, before one of them shoved her away, 'Go on, fuck off ou' of 'ere.' She made no sound at the ill-treatment, knowing the routine well enough, and departed without comment, not even a curse.

Hull left the sparring couple outside and entered the pub. He no longer recognised the interior since his drink with the doctor some weeks earlier. Smoke obscured the walls and tables so that the mass of bodies inside lost their individual outlines. His eyes burned and teared. He reached into his pocket, knowing that he had made a mistake in coming. It would have been wiser to have gone to bed, despite his foolish visions. He put a handkerchief to his eyes and turned to leave, when Fox waded towards him. 'Good fellow, you came. Drink this,' he said, holding out a tumbler of oily brown liquid.

'What is it?' Hull shouted over the noise.

'Home distillery. Excellent stuff. Nellie makes it herself. Get it down you, it's all in the spirit of the thing.' Then the smoke took him as he wandered off, calling, 'Back in a minute.'

Hull touched the liquid to his lips. It was foul, earthy, leaving his mouth numbed, his throat afire. He looked for a table to place the tumbler on, but could find none.

Each space seemed to be inhabited by customers standing, leaning, shouting, spilling drinks on the floor.

'Mind yourself,' said a man carrying three pint glasses, and Hull realised that he was still in the doorway. He moved off, pushing through the celebrants until he reached a spot where he could stand without obstructing anyone's comings and goings.

In a corner two men were playing fiddles, a third was blowing some kind of flute, hand-whittled. He was the most animated, a giant of a man, whose stamping legs added to the percussion. 'Play something from home,' called another man, approaching from the bar, dragging behind him a companion, who was barely conscious. He held the drunk up by his breeches, before turning towards the musicians and beginning to sing without their accompaniment:

You noble diggers all, stand up now, stand up now,
You noble diggers all, stand up now,
The wasteland to maintain, seeing cavaliers by name
Your digging do disdain and your persons all defame
Stand up now, diggers all.

He was solemn in his song, singing with full-throated ardour, his head tilted back. Passing men slapped him good-naturedly, staying to hear if the song would become bawdy. But their smiles faded when the lewdness did not arrive, when they were instead reminded of what had been taken from them in various ways in disparate places:

The gentry are all round, stand up now, stand up now,
The gentry are all round, stand up now.
The gentry are all round, on each side they are found,
Their wisdom's so profound to cheat us of the ground.
Stand up now, diggers all.

His audience walked away grimly, in search of lighter entertainment, and the musicians took up their instruments again in a rousing jig. Hull left too, finding with surprise that the beaker he had previously thought to abandon was now empty. He nudged past a billiard table where four men were occupied. Despite their jesting, a pile of dirty notes on the rim of the table suggested something more serious. Hull neared the bar and shouted to Alfred that he wanted water, receiving instead a beaker of alcohol like the first.

A short man, leaning with some difficulty against the bar, waved at Hull and lolled towards him. 'I wait, I wait,' he said. 'I think, no – he no come! But now you here – so!'

Hull shook his head. 'You're mistaken. I don't know you.'

The little man winked. He patted his breast pocket and ushered Hull aside, speaking low in a foreign language. Again the man patted his pocket, glanced around, before lifting out a handkerchief, shielding it from the room with his body.

'Helluvabeegwaan,' he said, showing Hull a hand formed into the shape of a bowl. But the handkerchief was empty. 'You like. You buy.'

Hull shook his head.

'You buy!'

'Bugger off, Kazankov,' said Fox behind them. 'He doesn't want your sodding diamond.' He put his arm around the magistrate as the man shuffled away. 'Poor chap, that one. Used to be an IDB out in Kimberley till he fell on hard times. Gets like this whenever he's had a skinful, you know. Now, how's your drink? Empty. Here's another.'

Hull accepted the tumbler, held it up a little as though about to toast, but thought better of it and took a sip instead.

'You wanted to meet Tregowning, didn't you? Let's see where he is. I saw him only a moment ago...'

They found the Cornishman leaning against a wall, watching the billiards game. He was older than Hull, his black beard peppered with grey, and he seemed to stand alone in the unruliness of the room, untroubled by it.

'Tregowning, this is Hull, the new magistrate. He's looking for a shooting instructor and whatnot. Someone to show him the lay of the land, you know. Has a passion for nature and all that. I said you're just the fellow for the job.'

'Pleased to meet you, Mr Tregowning.'

'Call me Jory.' Then, 'You can ride?'

Hull wavered. 'I can ride well enough, I suppose. But I must warn you that I have not done so in this sort of terrain before. And it has been some time, if I am honest, since I was last astride a horse.'

'Fine. You'll have to write a note to the stableman though. I'm in bad with Reid and he's banned me from borrowing from the stables.'

'Thank you, Mr Tregowning, but if that is the case—'

'Now, now,' said Fox, 'don't be so goddamn serious. Reid's a hot-tempered son of a bitch. Why don't you and Tregowning have a chat. I'll just get us some more drinks.'

Hull waited for the Cornishman to speak, but the man leaned on, watching the game. Hull drank deeply from his tumbler, tried to catch Tregowning's eye when two of the billiards players cheered at an opponent's failure. He drank again, draining the glass. 'What did you fall out with Reid about?' he said at last.

Tregowning sighed, pinched the bridge of his nose. 'The company handed out jackets to the natives for the cold – a few months ago now. They made it seem like a kindness. But they've been docking the workers' pay since then, far in excess of what those rags are worth.'

'But surely it is no more than a misunderstanding?'

'Not likely. They get taken advantage of – we all do – but the natives get the worst of it. I spoke to Reid about it and he didn't like that.'

'Perhaps he felt that it was not your place to do so.'

Tregowning turned to face the magistrate. 'Are we not taught to vindicate the weak and fatherless, to help the afflicted and destitute, to rescue the feeble and needy? To deliver them out of the hands of the wicked?'

Hull looked around uneasily. His tongue felt thick as he spoke. 'Some would call those revolutionary words.'

'I thought they were biblical.'

'Are they?' said Hull, though his voice seemed to be coming from elsewhere, his body to be dissolving beneath him. 'I must be muddled. I don't seem to... Yes, I'm muddled. I mud-must be.' He put his forehead against the cool sweat of the wall. 'I'm falling, I think.'

Tregowning gave a dry laugh. 'It's that concoction of Nellie's. Its deadly when it hits. Wait until tomorrow, you'll be shitting blood.'

'God,' said Hull. 'God.'

'Stay calm. Whatever you do, keep your eyes open. You'll be lost if you close them.'

'Good. Yes, I'll keep them open. Won't close them. You're kind. Very kind. You'll help me, won't you? You'll help me. I told Iris. Mrs McBride. I told her that I wanted to see more. You'll help me.'

Nearby, a man climbed on top of a table and bellowed, ''S an honour, privilege I say, t'be here – here – on this day. This day 'f all days. No better dog – no better—'

'Give it a rest!' another shouted, knocking the table so that the orator fell to the ground, crushing glass beneath him.

Hull leaned heavily against the wall. 'Keep your eyes open,' he said to himself. 'Open.' His head was akilter. The room shifting. From a far-off place a chorus had been taken up with the enthusiasm of the very drunk. It was being sung with swinging arms and impatient legs. Throughout the building the panic of laughter and shouting made way for words rendered now as nothing more than a continuous cry of 'Ay, ay!' A great din of noise and song spread through to the billiard table and bar, its rhythm guiding Hull ever closer to the blackness of sleep, as he dropped his head onto the Cornishman's shoulder, who repeated, 'Keep your eyes open. Open them. Open.'

It was still, the mine silent and grey in the morning. Drunks slept off the previous night inside the pub, while outside the streets were occupied by stray dogs and a litter of bottles and other cast-offs. Yet slowly Sunday rituals began to assert themselves. From the east, in the Village, a low hum of morning hymns came from the large tent where Waterboer's flock had already congregated. It echoed and advanced around the valley so that everything was hemmed in by song. The sound drove the town's inhabitants from their beds. They rose drowsily, readying themselves for service at the stone church. Men yawned and cursed as they dipped fingers into washbasins that had iced over during the night. Women threw shawls around their shoulders and rushed across brittle grass to outhouses as their long braids slapped against their backs. While, from the direction of the jail, a voice called after them, 'Turd shitty shit turdy turdy shitty shit!'

The idiot, Johnny-boy, born with no more brains than a talking parrot, was the culprit. Aged 19, he had already been locked up for three years, ever since the death of his old mam. When free, he had been a danger and a nuisance, wandering the mines, breaking down doors, taking what he wanted. At the general store he tried to pay with leaves, scraps of paper, handfuls of pebbles. He communicated with sounds that he knew – a donkey's bray, dog growl, bird chatter, and the few words that he had learnt over time: yes, no, Mam, hungry, Johnny-boy. Each spoken as though by a person with a mouth full of food. For some weeks he had been kept in the ordinary cells, but that morning Genricks had returned him to the locked room at the far side of the building where he usually lived. There he had a window, and a view of several homes, their yards and outhouses. He watched through the bars, announcing each time a person appeared, making known the time and frequency of their ablutions by his shouts.

With his cap pulled low, an ancient greatcoat fetid and heavy around him, Noki went towards those calls. Tengo walked beside him, wrapped in a cowhide. Solomon followed a little way behind, his arms bare, a large scarf covering the lower half of his face. Noki approached the window. 'Hello, Johnny-boy.'

The chant stopped and the idiot looked out at the three visitors through his narrow eyes. 'Johnny-boy,' he said.

'I've brought you something.'

Solomon came closer, holding out a foreleg from the duiker he had killed and roasted the previous night. Johnny-boy snatched for it, his fat moon face pressed against the bars, fingers stretching as he whined to have it. Solomon took another step forward until the leg was within reach. Johnny-boy grabbed it, pulled it towards himself, but could not work out how to bring it through the bars, making do with biting around them, the meat greasy against the metal, his teeth sharp on bone.

'Have you seen my brother?' said Noki. 'He should be wearing a red shirt and he's this tall.' He put a hand to his forehead. Then, 'Here, on his jaw, here, he has a scar. Do you know him? Have you seen him?'

Johnny-boy held out the stripped bone, said, 'Hungee.'

'No, there's no more. That's all.'

Johnny-boy pointed at Solomon. 'Hungee.'

'I gave you all of it. I don't have more.' He held out two empty hands.

Beyond the town's central koppie, the Anglican church bell began to toll, Main Street busying at the sound of it.

'Hurry up,' said Tengo.

Noki spoke quickly. 'Listen, Johnny-boy, listen please. Look at me. Can you give him a message? Anele, that's his name. Can you—'

'Hungee! Hungee! Hungee!' Johnny-boy shouted, shaking the bars.

'Shh, quiet, please, be quiet.'

By now people had stopped in the street. They stood in their Sunday best, turning their heads towards the back of the jail. In a nearby cottage a woman opened a window, calling to someone inside to come and see. Farther still, at the Residency, Genricks walked out onto the stoep to sweep, and shielded his eyes, looking towards the commotion. When he realised that it came from the prison, he threw down the broom and limped hurriedly to the building, yelling, 'You fucking kaffirs, what you up to? What you doing? I see you, you bastards, I see you.'

'We're not doing anything,' said Tengo, pushing Solomon behind him.

'Hungee, hungee!'

'What you done to him? I'll have you all in jail! I'll have you whipped! I'll have you beaten and bleeding!'

But Noki put his head back and called, 'Anele, can you hear me? Anele! Are you in there?'

Genricks sprang forward, grabbed Noki by the large collars of his greatcoat. 'You shut up, you shut the hell up, or it'll be me what shows you how.' He tried to move him, push him to the ground, but the jailer was weak against the miner's strength. Noki took Genricks' wrists, jerked them away from the coat, shoved him against the wall of the jailhouse. The jailer gave a cry, began to screech, 'Help! This kaffir's tryna kill me! Help, help!'

Noki placed a hand across Genrick's throat. 'Be quiet.'

By now a small crowd had gathered. Some of them laughed, others hissed at the jailer, booed his cries. 'Go on, kill him!' one of them shouted at Noki. 'Good riddance to him.'

But Noki only kept his hand loose around the jailer's neck, calling again for his brother. 'Anele! Anele! Say if you're there.'

He did not, at first, feel the hand on his shoulder, did not hear his name being spoken. When it was said a second time, he turned, saw the Cousin Jack behind him.

'Noki,' Tregowning said again, gentling his hand away from the jailer's neck.

'My brother.'

Tregowning looked across to where Genricks

97

grimaced, rubbing at his throat. 'You sack of shit. You still have Anele after all this time?'

'Who's a sack of shit? Who's a fucking sack of shit? Tell me, tell me, you sodding Cornishman!' The jailer leapt, grabbing him round the middle, knocking him to the ground. But Tregowning rolled him over, pushed his back into the dirt, held down his arms while the jailer kicked out and thrashed his head from side to side. He bared his teeth and made lunges at the Cornishman in an attempt to bite him. 'I ain't afraid of you, no I ain't.'

Someone yelled, 'Get him off! The bastard's trying to eat Tregowning,' and insults began to fall, the crowd in uproar as the men battled on the ground.

Again the church bell tolled, though no one heard. The crowd so loud that drunks began to stumble from the pub in query, and those who had not yet been roused from their beds came to windows and doors to find the source of the disturbance. The magistrate, his eyelids heavy in a pale face, left the Residency, wearing his dressing gown and a pair of slippers that slowed his walk through the sandy street. By the time he reached the scene, a man had pulled Genricks off the Cornishman, and another was shouting, 'You cannibal, fighting dirty like that.'

'Let him go,' said Hull. Then, 'What is the meaning of this, Genricks? What is all this about?'

'It weren't me, sir,' he said, pressing the back of a hand to his lip, checking for blood. 'I done nothing. It were that kaffir what started it all.'

'Which?'

Noki stepped forward. 'I only wanted to know about my brother, boss.'

'He is a prisoner?'

'Yes, boss.'

'If that is the case then you have acted wrongly. Men go to jail as punishment. You are not meant to pass messages to them. Their punishment is incarceration and denial of the outside world.'

'Yes, I understand, but—'

'No, that is all. There is nothing more to it.'

'No,' said Tregowning. 'That is not all. Let us sort this matter out now. Anele has been in jail for a long time. Too long. We want to know why.'

'What can you tell me on this matter, Genricks? Did I sentence this man?'

'No, sir. It were the previous magistrate. The boy's a drunk. Gave us a lot of trouble, he did. He's due for release next week.'

'There, did you hear that, boy?' Hull said. 'You will see your brother shortly. Now, on your way please, no more of this sort of behaviour. It will not be tolerated again.'

'This man is not honest. I do not believe him,' said Noki.

The magistrate breathed out. 'That is not for you to decide. You will do as I tell you or face the consequences.'

But still Noki did not move. He stayed, watching as Tregowning went up to the magistrate, spoke low. 'I urge you to look into this matter, Hull. He is right – Genricks is not to be trusted.'

'It ain't true, sir. He's a liar. A filthy, filthy liar.'

Hull held up his hand to silence the jailer. 'Mr Tregowning, I cannot allow you to say such a thing. It is you who cannot be trusted. I was warned that you are a troublemaker and here is ample evidence. Fighting in the street on a Sunday morning, like a common criminal. It is disgraceful. I thought to call you a friend, but I see now that that is not possible. Not with a man like you.'

'I don't care what you think of me.'

'No doubt you do not. By rights I should have you arrested for disturbing the peace. Please leave and take your companions with you. None of you is wanted here.'

'I am going, but if Anele Noki is not released next week then we will have this conversation again.'

The magistrate turned away and put out his hand to touch Genricks' arm. 'Are you hurt?'

'No, sir. Just rattled. They troublemakers, all right.'

'We'll keep an eye on them,' he said, watching as Tregowning and the others began to walk away. 'We must prevent such a thing from happening again.'

'That we must, sir.'

Hull sighed and took his hand from the jailer's arm, using it to gesture at the cell window where Johnny-boy had continued to chant and whine all this time. 'But why was this man placed here? It is clear that he is impaired. I think it is best for you to remove him to a windowless cell for the time being. I will speak to Dr Fox and see what can be done about transferring him to an asylum. In truth, I cannot understand why it has not been done before.'

Genricks shrugged. 'Mr Tweed had a personal likeness for Johnny-boy. Found him cheerful. Just did as I were told.'

Behind them the church bell tolled with increased vigour, and ahead the Baster hymns rose and rose.

Hull nodded. 'I know, Genricks. That is the best any of us can hope for, to do as we are told.'

The days had chilled considerably, though the heart of winter had passed. Hull found himself increasingly listless, isolated, bored. He kept indoors more than before, complaining to Genricks of the cold and the lack of variety in his meals. 'It's always the same now,' he said, leaving food untouched on his plate. 'When do things change?'

In his boredom, Hull several times considered having Tregowning sent for, thinking to be magnanimous and forgive him his behaviour. But always he baulked in the end. He would not be a man that begged for companionship, not of that sort anyhow. He did, however, write to Fox, mentioning that it was some time since they had last met and that he hoped the doctor might stop by when next he was in town. But that had been a week since, with no response.

Nothing satisfied Hull in his current mood and he became increasingly disgruntled by the weather, the out-of-the-way location, the raucous pub so near and the unfailing stupidity of the natives. He had let it be known that he would pay for interesting animal specimens, and within a few days the valley had been stripped clean. They came with handfuls of ants, chickens stolen from coops, dogs with their heads stoved in. One native had walked all the way from the port with a seagull rotting in an old flour sack. Another had sewn the head of a baboon to the body of a jackal, claiming it to be a rare creature that lived deep in the mountains.

'I won't see anyone else,' Hull told the jailer. 'Tell them all to go away. I don't want their wretched carcasses. Send them away, do you hear?'

His annoyance was at its height when a parcel arrived from Port Nolloth. Genricks brought it through to where Hull sat reading in his study one afternoon. 'It's the wool suit what you ordered,' he said, unwrapping the articles from the brown paper.

'But it's green!' Hull said in dismay. 'I asked for grey, did I not?'

101

'I believe as you did, sir.'

'Can nothing be done properly in this place? Must everything be a farce and a chore?'

'It can be difficult.'

Hull sighed and shook his head. 'Well, I suppose green will have to do. There's nothing to be done about it now. Help me on with it, would you?'

The jailer tugged and adjusted as best he could, but there was no helping the fact that the garments were ill-fitting, made to the measurements of a shorter, broader man. He fetched a bevelled mirror from the bedroom, tilting it so that the magistrate could take in his entire body. Hull saw bare ankles, lumpen shoulders. 'Dammit, this will never do for calling,' he said, pulling at the front of the jacket. 'I shall look a fool in it.'

'Was you planning a visit, sir?'

'Not planning exactly. But Mrs Townsend did invite me to come whenever I had the wish to do so, and she has recently written to reissue the invitation. It would not be polite to slight Mr Townsend and his wife.'

'Or their daughters.'

'Now now, none of that, Genricks. Help me off with these things. I declare I've lost my arm in here somewhere.'

The jailer slid the jacket from the magistrate, folded it carefully and placed it on the desk. He lowered himself on both knees and began to loosen the trousers. Hull pursed his lips. 'Listen here, Genricks, I know it was all in fun, just a little humour between ourselves, but I won't have people making jokes about myself and Mrs McBride. She is in mourning, you know.'

'Yes, sir. But, sir, they ain't saying aught about Mrs McBride. It's the other one what they been joking about. Word is she's been planning the wedding since afore you got here.'

Hull cleared his throat. 'Well, yes, well, certainly that is equally unacceptable. I won't stand for this sort of idle gossip.'

The jailer bowed his head. 'Yes, sir. Sorry sir.' Then, 'Have you decided? Will you be calling anywhere tomorrow? I only ask so's I know whether to polish your shoes.'

'Perhaps I will after all. Yes, I may do so if I find no pressing matters arise that require my attention.'

But the next afternoon did not find Hull inclined for calling. Instead he donned the ill-fitting suit and walked out into the neighbouring plains with his assistants, regardless of the fact that there was nothing of value left in them to inspect. He made the men walk up and down with him in endless lines, or else stand still for hours at a time, keeping them late in order to watch the first stars rise. Beside him they grumbled about the cold, even though he had gifted them with coats and gloves. Ned wore his happily enough, but Oupa found the gloves unnatural, saying that they turned his hands into those of a corpse, he could feel nothing with them. He continually flexed his fingers, bringing them up to his face, whimpering phrases that Ned translated as 'hands of the dead, touch of the dead'. At last Hull could stand it no longer and turned on the old man, ripping the gloves from him. 'They're alive again, you fool! You can stop your muttering! Your hands are alive, for God's sake!'

It continued in this way for a week, Hull returning from his excursions in a foul temper, swearing to Genricks as he undressed and bathed him that he was done with Hottentots. 'They are savage imbeciles. Nothing will ever transform them into anything otherwise. There is no hope for them. None at all. They can live in their ignorance and rot!'

Each night he went to bed in anger, more determined than ever to visit the Townsends the next day, to flee, for a few hours, the savagery of Springbokfontein and sit in a civilised drawing room with civilised people. Several times in the night he rose to pen letters to the Super, announcing his intended call, before tearing them to pieces half complete. Still, in wild moments he allowed himself to imagine that he might arrive at the Super's home and be told that everyone was out, that only Mrs McBride was able to receive him. He rehearsed topics that he might discuss with her about the natural world of Namaqualand. Such as the darkling beetles of the family *Tenebrionidae*, which tapped with their abdomens on the sand, a percussive song with which they attracted mates. He considered which specimens he could safely transport to Okiep by donkey cart for the amusement of herself and little George, and with which bulbs he might present them for planting. But then, always in those last moments before sleep was upon him, he recalled how reluctantly she had spoken to him, how her face had been turned away from him as though in disgust. No, he would not visit. He would not. He would stay here, here where he was trapped in his loneliness and isolation. He would see no one. He would be alone.

And then, at last, one night when he returned from another evening's expedition, clapping his hands and stamping his feet with the cold, he looked up to find Fox seated at the kitchen table talking to the jailer.

'Ah there you are, you mad devil,' Fox said. 'No doubt frozen to death. This weather is enough to brittle a man's bones, you know. It's kept me busy, I can tell you that much. Genricks, my man, pour two large brandies and bring them to us in the study by the fire.'

Hull followed the doctor and sulkily removed his scarf and gloves before settling back in an armchair with a frown, his black mood still upon him. He wanted to ask why the doctor had not come sooner, why he had abandoned him when the loneliness and the dark and cold were at their worst. He shuffled his toes back into life and made stars with his stretched hands before the fire, but said no word. Once Genricks had brought in the drinks, Hull took a large gulp and nodded as the jailer said his goodbyes for the night. After he had left, Fox leaned forward in his chair and said, 'Now listen, Hull, you needn't be so sullen, old chap. I know it's the winter that has you down and this maddening place. It happens to all newcomers. But listen, I have some good news. I have saved you a world of bother.'

'How so?'

'I don't know if you're aware of this, but you had a case on the books coming up this week. A nasty one. Infanticide, down in the settlement. Nothing left of the babe but its bones. There was talk of cannibalism and witchcraft, you know. I don't have to tell you what that would have meant. Christ. A witch hunt and lynchings and all sorts of unpleasant things. But I have just been out on a similar case in the Zulu camp. Little kaffir child dragged away in its sleep by a jackal or a leopard or something, had its arm ripped off before the parents managed to chase the creature off. It's the fat, you see, they lather the children in it for warmth and protection from insects and it's irresistible to the wild animals. Anyway, that's evidence enough, don't you think, in that other case? It can be dismissed now. Just a baby eaten by a wild dog and the bones left behind, no witchcraft at all.'

'Did the child survive?'

'Which, the one tonight? It lives yet, but I cannot say it will for long. It is likely dying as we speak. It's for the best, really. After all, what good is a one-armed man on the mines. Anyway, I can bring you the limb if you like; they found it not too far away, hardly a mark on it, all the little fingers still intact. You can bottle it up for your collection,' he laughed.

'That is uncalled-for. The child will die and you make jests.'

'Oh Christ, Hull, you're far too serious. You're growing quite dull. Do yourself a favour and visit one of Nel's whores for God's sake and have done with this foul mood once and for all.'

105

For days it rained. At times knuckle-sized hailstones fell, thundering on the iron roofs and smashing through windows. Very soon the dry earth was saturated. Rivulets ran across the sand, puddles formed. The main street was an endless mire in which the horses faltered, their hooves made gigantic by mud. Outside the pub, a spider-cart became stuck and it took eight half-drunk men to dislodge it, only to have it stick again a few yards away.

Even in the tunnels and caverns of the mine there was little respite from the rain. The beam pump, charged with pumping water out of cavities, had broken. Now water poured down the walls of the pit, snuffing candles, or else it welled up at ankle height, streaming unhindered.

The settlements were the worst affected. The very ground that the inhabitants slept on had turned to mud. Inside the shelters all was wet, the food soggy and fermenting. Diarrhoea was common and it flowed with the rain along the pathways between the shacks. There was no escape from it. Children played in it, men trudged through it with bare feet, or, if they had shoes, it soaked through cracks in the soles. These feet carried the waste into their homes where it slept and woke and went out into the world again to be added to. Dr Fox visited the settlements, tending to headaches, coughs, abdominal pain, nose bleeds. 'Boil the damn water!' he yelled. 'Keep dry and warm!' But they could only look at him blankly. The firewood was wet. The ground was wet. How could they boil anything? How could they hope to be dry?

Fox complained of it, his voice hoarse, when he called at the Residency again. Though it had been a week since their last meeting, Hull remained sullen. He had continued with his cases each morning, yet he felt dull, depressed. He did not have the same enthusiasm for his field work, and spent more hours than were healthy brooding in his armchair. He complained to Genricks that he was ill, demanding tea at all times of the day, then refused to drink it, saying it hurt his throat to do so. He began, too, to reject the lunch that the jailer now brought to him on a tray in his study. 'I'm not hungry,' he said, and once, when pressed, shouted, 'I don't want it, dammit!' bringing down his hand with such force that it knocked the tray and its contents to the floor.

This behaviour compelled Genricks to send for Dr Fox with some anxiety.

'He ain't well, you can see that, Doctor,' he said as he ushered the man into the magistrate's study. 'He just ain't what he was. Eats no more 'n a bite and barely stirs from this here chair.'

'Really, it is nothing. You needn't have come,' Hull said with a limp wave of his hand.

'It's no trouble at all, not at all. Now, Genricks, go make us some tea and I will inspect Mr Hull.'

Fox matched the magistrate's pulse to the ticking of his watch, looked at the pinks and whites of his eyes, peered in his throat. 'As I suspected. Nothing serious, old chap. Just a little head and chest cold, and perhaps a touch of melancholia brought on, no doubt, from overwork. You will have some discomfort, but it will pass soon enough. I can bring you some tincture for a purge, but I think perhaps the best thing for you is rest. Genricks will look after you. Set aside the cases for a while and relax in front of the fire, you know. Those who are waiting in jail can simply wait a little longer while you recover. It's a pity the rain hasn't passed otherwise you could sit outside, as you do enjoy being out in nature so very much.'

Hull sniffed.

'Ah, though perhaps it is better inside,' Fox continued. 'Outside is unpleasant. The stench is absolutely abominable. Those damned natives. It happens every year. Enteric fever. And before we know it it's a bloody epidemic. They will never learn.'

Hull looked up. 'An epidemic?'

'Don't worry, you're not in danger of getting it. Nothing for you but rest. I'll have Genricks boil up a healthful broth for you. And put tallow on your nose for the mucus. That always helps.'

Hull grunted.

'Right, let me be off for the moment. Take care of yourself, old chap. I don't want to have to report to the Super that you are unwell, you know. Drink plenty of fluids, but nothing that hasn't been boiled first. And make sure that you have an abundance of hot toddies,' he added with a wink.

Noki threw the dregs of his coffee on the ground and pulled his thin jacket close as he stepped out to join the trudging column of workers making their way through the drizzle to the open mouth of the Blue Mine. They walked with purpose, watching their breath whiten as it left their mouths. They needed no light to guide them. The dawn sky was enough to show the hulking rubble that surrounded the pit. Pile upon pile was revealed in the darkness as a many-humped beast casting its height over all. Up to now the creature had been asleep, but as the workers returned along green-stoned trails, the mounds began to wake. With the stuttering breath of a consumptive, the engines came to life, and within the beast, the internal organs, those tunnels and galleries of its innards, began to heat up so that it grew in height and depth and width.

Noki met Tengo, and together they slopped through the settlement towards the shelter of Moses. The evening before, the man had been coughing hard enough to stumble upon leaving the pit. No one had said anything. It was common in miners to develop a cough after less than a year, and Moses had been down the mines for much longer than that. Still, Noki felt uneasy about his friend, and though he nodded when Tengo said, 'He'll be well again this morning,' Noki remained uncertain.

When they reached the hut, there was no sign of Moses, only the boy waiting for them with a fist pressed to his mouth. Seeing the men approach, he gasped through his fingers, 'I don't know what to do. What can I do?'

Inside, Moses lay doubled over, his teeth clenched and eyes tight. There was a smell about him of sweat and sewage, his whole body damp, as though he had been soaked in both.

Noki crouched beside him. 'What is it? Tell me, what's the problem?'

But it was the boy who answered. 'He says it's something inside him. A pain. And in the night there was blood.'

'Blood? From where?'

'His nose and mouth, and some from behind. It's loose inside him.'

'Did you give him coffee? Something hot?'

The boy shook his head, bit at his knuckles. 'The wood is too wet. We haven't had fire for days. What's wrong with him? What can I do? Tell me what I can do for him.'

'Go to my hut and get some wood there. It's damp, but it will burn. You must make him some coffee,' said Tengo.

The boy looked out through the rain towards the minehead, where already a thousand or more people had gathered. 'The bell is going to ring soon. There's no time. There's no time now.' His voice rose, 'He won't want to be late. We can't be late. We have to go.'

'Then run quickly and see if anyone has any coffee left over. Be quick now.'

After the boy left, Noki and Tengo helped Moses into a sitting position. He held his stomach, said, 'It's the same fever that killed all those people in the Nama camp last year. I know it is.'

'No,' said Noki. 'You're sick because of the weather, that's all. You need some rest.'

'If I rest today, I'll rest every day. Reid doesn't care. He'll hire someone else and my family will starve. You know that. Don't pretend that you don't. Come, pull me up before we're late.'

Solomon returned with a half tin of bitter coffee. Moses drank it down, spitting out the grounds. His face hardened against the pain. He seemed another being then. Ceased to be a man, became instead a moving shape of rock and metal, as though the very ground had risen up around him and was now propelling him forward in the direction of the mine.

110

A crowd had gathered at the pithead. Mineworkers stood watching as voices rose nearby. By now the rain fell so heavily that Noki was unable to make out any words. 'What's happening?' he asked of another miner.

'Reid and the Cousin Jack.'

'Wait here,' said Noki to Moses and the boy. 'You don't want Reid to see you like this.' He and Tengo pushed a path through the gathered workers until they were able to see the two men standing very close to one another.

'It's dangerous,' Tregowning was saying. 'The groundwater has risen. The weight of it is too great. The earth is soaked. The pillars won't hold. There's no way they'll hold.'

'That's what the props are for.'

'There aren't enough props. You wouldn't let us have the timber.'

Reid pointed a finger. 'Watch yourself, Cornish. I do my job just as much as the next man. You watch yourself.'

'Look, there's no need for all this. I'm telling you it's not safe. It's just not safe. That should be enough. You must see that we can't go underground in these conditions.'

Around Noki the men began to grumble and shift uneasily as the bell commenced its ringing. The Cousin Jack was right, they murmured. The ground was sodden, the beam pump wasn't working. They whispered stories of mine accidents and collapses amongst themselves, each having heard of an incident more destructive than the first.

An American, Jenkins, called out, 'Tregowning has a point there, Reid. The walls aren't what they should be, and the water keeps rising. It isn't stable, not enough. We should listen to him. He knows better than anyone how mines work.'

Men nodded, voiced their agreement. No man understood mining as the Cornishman did, and none could compare with his knowledge and skills. He kept to himself, it was true, and he had his own ideas, but he knew what he was about and the miners respected him. Each man had

111

heard at least a version of Tregowning's past, that past in which at the age of 15, with mines closing across all of Cornwall, he had begged passage aboard ship to what some people still called the New World, and worked his way to Michigan where he got a job in a recently sunk copper mine by simply giving his surname to the Cornish mine boss, who had winked at him and whispered, '*Onen hag Oll*': one for all. When that mine too ran dry, he made for Australia, ending up at a tin mine in the northern territory. After seven months he fell out with the mine manager over dangerous practices. It was the same way at the other four mines he tried on that continent. He was proud about mining, about the right ways to do it, and could not abide shortcuts, nor the class of men hired to work beside him. 'You could rake hell with a fine-toothed comb,' he had told one mine boss, 'and come up with a better lot than this.' Having made a bad name for himself in that land as an upstart and troublemaker, he had sailed for the Cape.

'Listen to him, Reid,' a man called. 'You haven't been down there. You don't know what it's like.'

'That's right, you don't know. The Cousin Jack, he knows what he's talking about,' said another.

'Don't you lot start,' Reid said. 'Don't you dare start. He might be a Cornishman and think he knows mining through and through, but last time I checked the pay book it listed Frank Reid as manager of this mine, not Jory Tregowning. So I say what goes and you listen.'

The men looked across at Tregowning, but he would not return their glances, his eyes fixed on the mine boss. 'Don't you do it, Reid. For Christ's sake, don't do it.'

But, 'The bell's rung. You're all late,' said the manager. 'You lot better get down there or by God you'll be sorry! There's plenty who will work if you won't.'

That threat having been spoken, there seemed to be no more question on the matter. They did as they had been told, making their way to the shaft, quietly murmuring their displeasure as they began to pile down the ladder.

Behind them, the women and children separated towards their different areas, whispering behind hands made cold and soft by the falling rain.

Noki went across to where Tregowning remained standing. 'Come, boss, let's go. He's a bastard, but we have to do as he says or we have nothing.'

But before he could answer, Reid had advanced on them. 'Cornish, take your men to F chamber. There's been a rock fall and it's blocking the chute to the ore bins. You're so concerned with rock falls and cave-ins, now's your chance to do something about it.'

Tregowning eyed the man angrily, water dripping heavily from the brim of his hat. For some moments he did not move, nor did the mine manager.

'Please, boss, let's go,' said Noki again. 'Work is work.' And Tregowning dropped his gaze, began walking towards the mine entrance.

'On second thoughts,' Reid's voice came across the pithead, 'I don't think you need quite so many men, do you, Cornish? Clearing that rock won't take so long and it's not such an important job that you need three workers. You,' he said, pointing at Tengo, 'report to the beam pump. It needs fixing.'

As he lowered himself into the chute, Tregowning said, 'There will be blood on your hands, Reid. This mine will collapse and you will be to blame, you can count on that.'

'And I'll be having a word with the Super about you, you can count on that. Come tomorrow you'll find yourself out of a job, Cornish. I don't care if you're the last Cornishman alive. You're finished here.'

The pithead was empty. Noki and Moses alone remained. Moses was pale, bent slightly forward as he held his middle.

'This pain.'

'I'll go first,' Noki said. 'Follow me, I'll help you.'

The rungs of the ladder were wet and rough under-hand as he climbed down. All along the rock wall water was running thickly, carrying with it the stench of waste. Noki turned his face upwards and steadied Moses' legs with his right hand even as mud from the man's feet fell onto his face. He spat, but did not let go.

'Good, now bring down your left leg. That's it. Are you holding on? Good. Now your right leg. There. Now bring your hands down onto the next rung. Have you got it? Are you holding on? So, bring down your left leg. Left one, there you go.'

In this fashion they proceeded, gradually descending one rung at a time. It was slow, requiring many pauses when the pain became too much. Moses stopped, clung to the ladder, cried out. His legs shook and were only kept from slipping by Noki's steady hand. 'Come, it's not far. It's close now.'

The Blue Mine was shallow yet as far as underground mines went, and comprised two levels alone, requiring a descent of only 1,000 feet to reach the second level. They had already passed, blinkingly, the stretch of pale light that marked the first level, before continuing down into the blackness. Now, at last, yellow lamplight began to grow beneath them. At the final rung, Noki helped Moses down into the amber glow of the main entrance chamber of the second level, allowing his friend to lean against the wall as he scanned the cavern for Tregowning.

The Cousin Jack was talking to Jenkins while they lit their candles from an open-flamed lamp. The American was loud in his contempt of Reid, naming the man a bastard, a coward, an idler. Tregowning walked away, scowling. His frown deepened as he saw the haggard face of Moses. He lit the candles on the hats of the two natives and said, 'Come on, boys. Noki, get the tools and put them in the tub. I'll be doing the pushing for now.'

They followed Jenkins' group into the west passage. Jenkins continued to curse Reid and the Super as they waded through running water. The way was narrow and the men had to walk in single file. Though the tub was empty, it was awkward in the flooded tunnel. It regularly stalled and twisted, knocked into the rock walls on either side. The wheels squealed on unlubricated axles, growing tighter and more stubborn as the water increased around them. Noki came last of all, his hand on Moses' back to keep him steady and moving. Despite having walked these tunnels many times, Moses was stumbling, more than once dropping to his knees. The second time Noki pulled him up, he saw blood coming from his nose. He wiped it with his wet sleeve, leaving a line across Moses' lip and cheek.

Ahead of them Jenkins' team was turning off. By this time the American had stopped complaining. With each step inwards he had resigned himself more to his task, so that now his anger had turned to irritation and he shouted at Tregowning, 'Make haste with clearing that rubble. It's a long walk back to the main chamber, pushing tubs. We need that chute.'

'We'll do our best, but the whole place is falling apart.'

'Come on, aren't you always saying a mine is a living thing? A rock fall here or there is normal.'

'You know that's not the case now. I've just listened to you grousing about it all the way down here. I've seen you feel the walls. You know they're crumbling. This is not a living thing. It's dying.'

'Look, just clear the rubble quick as you can. There's more than just you working down here, all right?'

'Yeah,' was all Tregowning replied, and the other man turned away with a shake of his head.

It was three miles from the main chamber to the site of the rockfall. Moses was moving slower and slower, holding onto the sides of the tunnel as he went. Around them the air staled and heated. Soon the tunnel had shrunk to such an extent that the men had to crawl through the water, their heads low to keep from knocking them on the rock above.

'Go,' Noki said. 'Keep going.'

But in front of him the sick man sank again. His torso splashed down into the flow. He gave a moan, spitting water, and jerked with pain as Noki pulled him up.

Ahead, the Cousin Jack stopped. He turned. 'Come here,' he said.

Moses moved forward slowly. 'I'm sorry, boss.'

'You're unwell. You shouldn't be at work.'

'Please, I must work—'

'You can't work. Come, come here. Lie in here and rest.' He pointed at a small hollow in the side of the tunnel. 'The water hasn't reached this height yet and we're far enough that no one'll see you. Come on, get inside. That's it. Here, use my jacket as a pillow. Are you warm enough?'

'Yes, oh yes, boss. Thank you, boss.' Noki saw something previously inflexible relax in Moses' face.

'Now snuff that candle. Don't let anyone see you. We don't need Reid hearing about this.'

'I won't. I'll be quiet, I swear. Thanks, boss. Thanks.'

Half a mile later, Noki and Tregowning reached the entrance to F chamber. The tub thumped against rock as the Cousin Jack gave it a final push, and then the men unfolded themselves from their hunched positions, testing their heights, stretching their limbs. Tregowning took a candle from his pocket and lit it from the flaming wick of the one in his hat. He held it out before him, moving it around to cast light across the cavern. The rockfall was directly ahead of them, blocking the passage that led to the ore bins. He stepped over dislodged rocks, holding the candle aloft. 'It's not so bad. Look, it only covers half of the mouth of the passage,' he said. 'Bring the tub, Noki. We can get this done quickly enough, even if there are only the two of us.'

Noki manipulated the cocopan over the rock-strewn ground and removed the picks and hammers, handing one of each to Tregowning. Against the chamber walls his shadow repeated the action, large as a giant, while the Cornishman held his candle out over a protrusion on the rock wall and let four drops of tallow fall on it before pressing the candle in place. On the other side of the passage Noki did the same with a candle taken from inside his shirt. It took a moment to light, the flame small and sputtering, but once it was burning the cavern filled with an eerie yellow darkness.

They began first by lifting the loose, smaller rocks and hoisting them into the tub. When it was full, Noki pushed it back along the tunnel they had come from, pausing long enough beside Moses to see that the man was fast asleep. Returning from the main chamber where he had traded the full tub for an empty one, he stopped again. Moses was awake and called to him softly at his approach.

'How are you feeling?' Noki asked.

'Hot, but the pain is not as bad as before. I'm very thirsty. Do you have some water? I finished mine.'

'Here, take my canteen. I'll fill it on my next trip up.' Then, 'It's rising,' he said of the stream at his feet. 'I'm sure it's risen an inch or more this morning. Make sure that you keep clear of it, don't lie here and get wet.'

'No, I can get up now. I'm ready to work. I had a good rest.' Moses made to stand, but Noki laid a hand on him, pushed him back down.

'Stay and rest some more. There isn't much work to be done. The Cousin Jack said so himself. We'll be finished soon. It's better for you to stay here. Tomorrow you can work again.'

Noki pushed on towards the yellow light of the chamber and the sound of pick on stone. Already a gap had been made into the passage. He thought that five more tubs would see them finish, perhaps six, by which time Moses would have rested, recovered a little. He whistled to himself, giving a tune to his relief. Tregowning looked across at him as he approached, 'All good?'

'All good.'

Then a strange wave washed over Noki's feet, rising above his shins, and a low rumbling from above grew steadily louder until rock began shedding down on the two men in larger and larger fragments.

'Get down!' the Cousin Jack yelled, and Noki huddled himself in beside the cocopan, his hands covering his head as the ceiling collapsed around him. The sound of it split his ears, a thundering growl that shook his brain and stayed there, vibrating. After a while he began to feel that the noise had dulled outside, that it was living in his head alone. He wondered if he was deaf now and what life would be like for a deaf man. To communicate with pointing fingers, nods and shakes of his head, with words he would not be able to hear himself speaking, as all things buzzed inside him. But slowly, he began to discern the tinkling of small stones dropping, the sound of himself coughing, and he looked up into a world dark as pitch. He lifted his arms from his head, scattering gravel, and felt around him, his fingers brushing across a barrier of rocks, shoulder-height, that pressed his crouching frame against the tub. He pushed them from him and began to claw his way in the dark, his head still roaring as he called, 'Cousin Jack! Jack!'

He heard a seemingly faraway reply, 'Here, I'm here,' and crawled over the debris as Tregowning continued to call him closer. When his hand touched the other man's booted foot, he found himself laughing. To be touching a man's boot in the dark while he was going deaf. To be touching a man's boot. It seemed ridiculous. And he thought of the diamond miners he had met on his journey home. Of the man who had taken the boots and exchanged them for beer, and of the other one. The man with the hat. Were they still alive, those men?

'Help me,' Tregowning said. 'There's a rock on my arm. I can't get it off.'

Noki groped around until he found the rock, lifting it unsteadily, as the Cousin Jack wrenched his arm free with a cry. 'Christ, I think it's broken.'

Then the dim sound of scratching and fumbling reached Noki's ear, and after a few moments Tregowning said, 'Here, I have some matches. Light a candle, would you? I can't do it.'

Noki took off his hat and, from the crumpled matchbox that was passed to him, ignited a match, lighting the broken stub of tallow on the brim.

The cavern floor was gone, hidden under rocks that seemed to have grown up out of the ground at a supernatural pace. They enclosed the tunnel to the ore bins, and, outside the passage in which Moses slept, they lay as though purged, as though the passage had erupted before flattening in on itself.

Noki struggled forwards, getting as close as the fallen rocks would allow. 'Moses!' he yelled, but his voice hardly sounded through the thick air. 'Moses! Moses!'

'He won't be able to hear you. The whole first level of the mine has collapsed on us. He's probably dead.'

'We're not dead.'

'No, but we have an open space here, he has none. Just that small tunnel. It was completely crushed. If he isn't dead yet, he will be soon. There'll be no air for him to breathe.'

'But to die like that. Under all this. It isn't right.'

'It's the way of the mines; you should know that well enough. How many old miners do you see walking around?' As he talked, Tregowning began using his left arm to pull away the rocks from the tunnel that led to the ore mines. 'None. No miner sits by the fire in his old age with his grandchildren bouncing on his knee. It's the same for all of us. We die because of one of four things: cave-ins, lungs, brawling or strike. That's it. That's the four horsemen of the apocalypse. One of them for every mining man I've ever known, my grandfather and father included.' He looked back at Noki. 'We can grieve for Moses later. Now we must think of ourselves.'

Noki began clearing the debris. After some time they had made a hole large enough to crawl through. The tunnel was less badly affected than the passage that had claimed Moses. It existed still to a certain extent, allowing them to scramble over and around smaller rockfalls, shifting stone where necessary, until they reached a heavy, solid slab that could not be moved. It obstructed the entire passage, except for a thin gap at the top, the size of a slot in a letter box. They could go no further.

'So, here we are. Which of your four horsemen will it be for us?' Noki asked.

Tregowning put his head in the air and sniffed. 'It won't be a cave-in, I can tell you that much. It's about 800 feet to the surface. If we stay here they will find us. We just have to wait.'

'I gave my water to Moses,' Noki said.

'Are you thirsty? I have some. Here, have a little. We need to save it as best we can. It may be days yet before they reach us.'

Noki took a small sip and swilled it around his mouth

to clear the grit from his tongue. He swallowed it slowly, separating it into three parts. Each time he swallowed, his throat hurt. He coughed.

'I'll blow out the candle now,' Tregowning said.

They sat in the darkness, only a small sliver of grey coming down towards them from the distance above.

Hull was asleep when the collapse occurred. He was woken by the crash of a glass of water from his bedside table onto the floor. His bed shuddered under him and the wardrobe doors agitated on their hinges. A framed self-drawn sketch of a male Genetta tigrina fell off the wall, its glass shattered. Rumbling came from every side of the house. Mistaking it for the beating of war drums, he climbed out of bed to pull on his trousers. But as he stumbled into his shoes, the sound ceased, and he drew aside the curtain just in time to see a horse and rider shoot past in the direction of Okiep. Rain was falling heavily, the near surrounds a spattering of mud as wholly unpeopled by an army of invading savages as any other day.

He hastened out onto the stoep to find the cause of the tremors, seeing with alarm that men and women were running out of every building towards the mine. One woman slipped and fell in the mud, but no one stopped to help her up, and she struggled to stand up on her own. Screaming and wailing sounded across the town as native women dashed from the settlement. Some of them were barely covered, others had babies tied to their backs or small children trailing after them. From where he stood, Hull could see that the silhouette of the mine had changed entirely. Where before there had been mounds and piles, there now appeared to be only low-lying rubble. The Blue Mine seemed to have fallen inwards. Even the slag heaps had sunk downwards, and in place of the beam pump there now stood nothing.

He grabbed his umbrella from the stand beside the front door and hurried out, opening it with some difficulty as he made his way through the mud of the street. Ahead of him he saw Fox and Genricks coming out of the prison building. 'What is it? What's happened?' he called.

'There's been a cave-in at the mine,' Fox said, turning only slightly.

'Oh, good God! All those men. What can be done?'

Genricks opened his mouth, but it was again Fox who

spoke. 'Riders have been sent to Okiep. They'll bring men to help dig them out. In the meantime, every man above ground will do his bit. Reid is organising teams. We're on our way there now. There's no time to lose.'

'Yes, of course,' Hull said, joining the two men as they hastened onwards. He clutched his umbrella in both hands and tried to manoeuvre it in such a way that each of the other men might receive some protection from it.

'No, Mr Hull,' said Fox, putting out his hand to stop the magistrate's advance. 'You are unwell. You had best return to bed.'

'But surely every man—'

'This is Company business. Leave it to us. Go back inside. You are not wanted.'

Hull stood back. 'Come now, there are men in danger. I must, surely, be of some assistance. Genricks, what do you say?' he asked when the doctor made no response.

'Best leave it to us, sir, as the doctor says. It ain't no place for a magistrate. But I'll ask permission to assign the prisoners to digging, sir.'

'Of course. Do what you feel is best.'

'Yes, sir. I will. And you go back to bed now, sir.'

Hull wiped the tallow from his nose and did not go back to bed as he had been instructed to do. Instead he climbed onto a stool and returned the damaged sketch to its place on the wall. Afterwards he went down on his hands and knees to pick up the shards of glass, adjusted the cupboard doors, one of which had swung open, and began a half-hearted attempt to make his bed. For a while he stood at the window, looking out from behind the heavy green velvet curtain. People were shouting, racing past the cottage and away. Men from the settlement were carrying picks and spades, women hauled buckets. Others carried planks of wood, some with what looked to be parcels of dynamite tucked under their arms. Some women thronged with blankets that became soaked immediately in the downpour, while horses and riders weaved through it all, splattering mud. Somewhere a child bawled and Hull's fingers twitched at the sound, before pulling the curtain to.

In the study he inspected his displays for signs of damage, before struggling for half an hour to light a fire with his own hands. At its eventual burning, he sat in an armchair and opened his notebook, which he had not looked at for some time. Initially he read his notes fitfully, raising his head at each fresh yell, every horse's whinny that came from outside, but soon he became invulnerable to the noise, allowing it to fall into the distance as much as he did with the nightly revelling at the pub.

In recent weeks his fieldwork had resulted in the discovery of a charming little frog. He reread his records on the subject, making a note in the margin that the frog was more than likely from the family *Brevicipitidae* as it appeared to live underground and come out after rain to mate and feed. There was no webbing on its feet, which was in accordance with his belief that it lived always away from water. The males, he had observed, made high-pitched calls when in search of a mate. In fact, it was their mating and continuation of life that he found the most fascinating. When once they found one another, the frogs embraced and began to burrow underground. He had not been able to ascertain what happened from there, having discontinued his research during his illness, but he intended to resume his study the next day. He called for the jailer with excitement. 'Genricks! Genricks, where are you? I want you to prepare my things for tomorrow.'

But then he recalled the collapse, the miners trapped underground, and he heard again the chaotic toing and froing outside. In the grate the fire had gone out and the room was cold and dark. He was on his own. There was no one to place his clothing at the ready, to light his lamps or make his tea.

All night men rode in from the mines at Nababeep and Okiep. A farmer from Driegat Plaas came with four sons and six oxen. There was word that German volunteers would be arriving with the mule train from the Mission at Steinkopf, though they could not be expected until the following day. From further abroad, at the port, the unemployed were encouraged to make the journey to the Blue Mine and offer their assistance in exchange for payment. They piled onto the train, though perhaps their interest lay more in the dead than in money. Dead miners meant that positions would be available where before there had been none. Even the Namaqua Copper Company at Concordia sent a small convoy of men; enough that should one of their mines ever collapse, the CCMC would be obliged to send assistance in return.

Fires smoked blackly on the slag. The rain at least had stopped, bringing some sense of relief. Yet the mud continued to hamper rescuers in clearing rubble and digging into the mine. It caused them to slip, locked stones in place, made the ground dissolve at every attempt to catch hold of it in any way. Picks skidded from the rocks, shovels became little more than paddles in the water-laden ground, while any breaches collapsed immediately under the weight of the mud. For hours there had been a frenzy of digging, but as morning dawned on the second day, it became clear that no progress was being made. Reid called a halt and gathered the leaders for a meeting. 'To continue like this is fruitless. We need to decide where the best places are to dig and focus our attentions on them. We can't go on like this; we're getting nowhere.'

'Why bother? They're all dead,' said a mud-covered man, leaning on his shovel in exhaustion.

'We can't be sure of that. Company says we dig, and that's what we'll do.'

Another spat on the ground. 'All right, so we dig, but where? That's an entire mine that's been destroyed. Miles of it. How can we guess where they are? The whole shape of the mine has changed. It's impossible.'

Reid gestured at the debris, his voice loud as he sliced the landscape with his arms. 'From now on we dig down every 500 yards. That way we'll miss nothing. Pass the word on, will you? Tell everyone to dig at regular intervals. Tell the bloody natives too. They're making a right mess of it all. God be good and let the earth swallow them up and spit out our men instead.'

He returned to the shed that served as his office, and drank from a half-jack of Cape Smoke, glaring through the doorway at the chaos. He cursed the damned Super who had not bothered to come himself, who had done nothing in the face of this calamity, nothing but send a rider with a hastily scrawled note. *Dig them out. No more than seven days. Can't spare the expense.*

Though the new course for the rescue had been set out, excavation continued haphazardly. Attention was given to those few places where the earth allowed itself to be opened. From time to time a man would pause in his work to tap a rock with a stone, the members of his team shushing one another as they listened for a response. None came. Not until the fourth day, when all were raw from the dirt, their eyes streaming with lack of sleep, was the tap-tap-tap returned. Fifteen men, still alive. Rescuers broke through to them on the following afternoon, the miners covering their eyes against the candlelight that was now upon them. They crawled out with difficulty, some of them having to be dragged. In the mud, they groaned, wept, begged for water, speaking of the certainty with which they had awaited death. Some had their boots cut off, so swollen had their feet become, while the bare feet of the natives had paled and shed into frightening slabs.

Reid drank all the time now, taking sips in full view of anyone who cared to look his way. But the liquor did not hinder his speech, and he demanded of the miners, 'Are there others down there? Have you seen them? Did you hear anyone?'

The responses were garbled, though all spoke of the same thing, confirming that yes, there were others down there, near to where they had been, but none alive. That was certain. They had smelled them rotting, the stink of them tainting the water all around so that they had been unable to drink it.

The dead did not weigh on Reid. Why should they? He had done nothing wrong in sending them underground, no matter what the Cornishman had said. Still, he was angry. Angry that this had come to pass, and that the blame would fall on him. Already he had been abandoned by the Super, left to sort out the mess on his own. He took another swig from the bottle. Then another.

'All right, keep digging,' he said. 'Bring up the bodies if you can. Leave the kaffirs. We don't need their carcasses. Conserve your energy.'

But the dirt of the mine had rendered all men dark-skinned, and the corpses were brought up without stopping to determine what colour they might be. They were dragged to the flat terrain of the sorting field, where it became the job of others to separate them by race. A single man walked up and down the rows of the white miners, identifying them and recording their names in the pages of a ledger. On the far side of the area, the natives had been left in disarray. No one wrote down their names or prevented family members from carrying them back to their homes.

In the days after the collapse, Hull busied himself within the grounds of the Residency. Hoping to discover a mating pair of *Brevicipitidae* frogs, he excavated wherever the earth looked as though it might have been disturbed. Nearby he had a jar at the ready should he find them, and in his study he had prepared a vivarium for the eggs. Once placed in the glass case, he would be able to observe their growth and development, determining how they managed an existence almost entirely underground. However, digging was proving to be a trying business. The earth was little but sludge in places, and Hull haunched his way across the yard, until his thighs burned and he toppled backwards. He tried to stand, rolling first onto his knees, but the stiffness in his legs was so great that he chose to move forward in a crawl instead, caring little for his trousers' dirtied knees or the edges of his jacket that trailed in the mud. He found at last an area of soil that appeared to be drier than the rest. Here he could dig at his pleasure, the sand grains rasping against the trowel blade as he did so.

When, some time later, he looked up from his work, he was startled to find Mrs McBride and her son standing several yards away, watching him. She wore her veil again, and the boy had on a little straw boater that left his face in shadow. He was fiddling with a button on his jacket, the other hand holding onto his mother's skirts.

'Mrs McBride, I – this is a surprise. That is to say, I had not expected...' He gathered himself to his feet with some difficulty, wiped his brow with a dirty hand.

'We came with Dr Fox. Kitty wanted to see the rescue operation and my father felt that it would be beneficial for George to do the same.'

'Mr Townsend did not come himself?'

'No, he did not.' She paused, looked down at her son. 'The two of us find that we do not enjoy the rescue as an entertainment. We hoped to find a quiet place to wait, but the hotel appears to be closed.'

'Of course, yes. Well, you are most welcome to wait

in the Residency until Miss Townsend is ready to leave. I am afraid I am quite muddy at this minute, as you can see, but you're most welcome to go inside and make yourselves comfortable.'

'Thank you. May I ask in what it is that you're engaged? We have been observing you for several minutes and have been unable to guess.'

Hull laughed a little. 'Yes, I am sure I must make quite a sight. I am searching for a charming little frog in order to study its habits.' He recalled his imagined conversations with Mrs McBride, the rehearsed words that might impress her. 'You know, I send all my findings to the museum in Cape Town for classification. I have sent many that were not yet known to man. And I am not paid for my time. The formaldehyde, jars, shipment, all of it comes out of my own pocket. That is my personal contribution to history. Perhaps I am not as heroic as others,' he gestured in the direction of the mine, 'but there is more to me than a magistrate's robe.'

She nodded, a little stiffly he thought, and so he rushed on nervously, 'Oh yes, it is in the natural world that I truly find the most joy, just as you mentioned to me once before about your own delight in nature. It really is extraordinary that there can be so much life under our feet. We tread on it daily, not realising that beneath us hearts are beating.'

George released his hold of his mother's skirts and walked towards Hull. 'Frog,' he said quietly. Then louder, 'Frog.' He crouched down and put a hand into the hole that the magistrate had been digging. He took Hull's trowel and began to use it in the wet soil. Again he said 'Frog', and spoke a sentence that they could not understand.

'I hope George is not interfering with your work, Mr Hull.'

'No, no indeed.' He knelt beside him, showing him where to dig. The boy unearthed a beetle and held it up for inspection. 'Very good,' said Hull, dropping it into the jar. George wandered over and watched the jar for a while, and another beside it which held worms and grubs. Then he returned to his digging, talking quietly to himself.

'I am afraid he is getting very dirty,' said Hull.

'I do not mind that. I am happy for him to be engaged in any activity that takes him away from the mines.' She had lifted her veil and seated herself upon a rock.

'You do not care for mining.'

'No, I do not. I spent many years at Okiep, and marriage took me away from the mines to other mines and mining companies on different continents. I have seen enough to believe that there is nothing admirable in them.'

'In the industry, you mean?'

'That, but more so in what it does to a man. No man can survive a mining town without being corrupted and weakened by it. All feeling for his fellow man is lost. He is scarcely human any longer.'

'If that is your belief, then, you will forgive the impertinence I hope...'

'Please, say what you wish.'

'I am only curious as to why, if you have such antipathy towards mining, why marry a mining man?'

Her eyes were downturned as ever. 'I was led to believe he had given up any interest in the mining business. I was led to believe many things.' She was silent for a moment, then turned her gaze on him and said, 'But what value is there in speaking with subtlety and excuses? I married out of desperation, Mr Hull. That is the long and short of it. And I suffered for it, I assure you, though I cannot say that I would not do the same again.'

'Then you did not love your husband?'

'I did not. No doubt you consider that immoral, but he understood the arrangement. I was honest with him from the beginning, which is more than he ever was with me. So, you see, I am not quite as bad as some might have you believe.'

'No. Not in the least. Not at all. You are the very opposite of that, I assure you. You are very much... I mean

131

to say...'

She looked away from him again. 'Did you find something, Georgie? What have you got there? Shall I help you?' Then, 'Have you another trowel, Mr Hull?'

'Of course. One moment.' But when he returned she and the boy both had their hands in the dirt. She laughed at the proffered tool. 'It is too late now, I think. We saw a worm and tried to dig it out, but it seems to have escaped us.'

He smiled. 'I am afraid I am not much of a host. I seat you in the dirt and am not even able to offer you tea. I am without my man at present and I do not know how to work the big coal stove. Indeed, I have been living on water and buttered bread for the better part of a week.'

'Oh, Mr Hull.'

'Yes, I cut rather a pathetic figure.'

'You are always welcome to come and have tea with us. Mama did write, did she not, to remind you that you might come?'

'Yes, I had intended to. But I was unwell, and then I did mean to come, only I wasn't able.'

'If it is dry biscuits that you are worried about, you needn't be,' she laughed. 'The ship has at last brought the consignment of fruit that we ordered, and now you can expect to be fed all those jam tarts you were deprived of before and that Kitty has been crying over ever since.'

Twice this day she had laughed in his company and he found that it brought something very pleasing to her face and voice. He tried to think of a humorous response, to make her laugh again, but he was ill at ease and could only manage, 'A little slower, if you please, Mrs McBride. You might damage any specimens that you come across if you continue to dig in such a violent manner.'

'Oh, I am terribly sorry,' she said, reducing her pace at once, leaving him to feel a fool, certain that she thought him a prig and a bore. Yet when he glanced across at her and the boy, both faces were broad with smiles.

Shadows lengthened across the yard and a cold wind swept through the valley.

'I don't suppose we will find the frogs today,' Hull said. 'I will try again tomorrow.'

He led Mrs McBride and George to a pail in which rainwater had collected. They took turns dipping their hands into it, and Mrs McBride wet her handkerchief to wipe the boy's face. She dried her hands on the folds of her dress, while Hull shook his, taking care to turn away from her as he did.

Fires had been lit at the mine and it was towards these that the three of them now slowly made their way.

'Thank you, Mrs McBride, and you too George, for your assistance today. It is a long time since I enjoyed myself to such an extent.'

'We enjoyed ourselves too. In fact, might we, if I may be so bold, might we return tomorrow? Georgie would dearly like to see the frogs. There is so little else for a young boy to do here, and this afternoon has been unexpectedly pleasant.'

'Of course. Yes, certainly. Truly, you would be very welcome.'

They found Fox and Genricks at the door to Reid's shed, the doctor's head back in laughter. He turned, smiling, at their arrival. 'Good evening. Good evening.'

'Dr Fox, I hope I haven't kept you waiting,' said Mrs McBride. 'I had not realised how late it was. Where is Kitty?'

'Goodness, she left hours ago. She said it was tedious and that the dirt was ruining her dress. I see the dirt doesn't worry you.'

'We fell,' she said, her former coldness returning to her. 'We all did. Is that so shameful?'

'No, of course not. Of course not. Had a little fall did you, Georgie? Never mind, I'm leaving now and we'll get you home to a nice bath and clean bed.' He waved at the mine. 'Not much more I can do here anyway. They're most likely all dead by now.'

'Do you think so?' said Hull. 'That is a great loss, a great loss indeed. I am very sorry to—'

'Why, Doctor,' interrupted Mrs McBride, pointing to a group of rescuers some distance away, 'who are those unfortunate men?'

'Prisoners.'

Hull turned hastily to take in a small group of men nearby. He drew back at the shock of what he saw. The men were horribly emaciated, clad in rags, and buckling under the weight of the rocks they were being made to haul. 'Good God, you cannot be in earnest! Those men are from the prison?'

'You gave permission, sir,' said Genricks.

'Permission for this? My God, my God, man.'

Her eyes were on him now and he felt himself to be again on that tipping cabin aboard the *Namaqua* with his torso exposed. He put a hand to his chest, felt the assurance of his clothing. Still, he was certain that he had never before been more naked as she asked, 'Those are your men, Mr Hull?'

He shook his head, murmured, 'Genricks.'

'What's the problem?' said Fox.

Louder now, 'Genricks, come here at once.'

'Yes, sir, here I am. I'm afeerd you been wanting me, you been alone, fending for yourself with not a soul what can take care of you.'

'Be quiet. You will take the prisoners back to the prison immediately. Have them waiting for me in the yard. I am inspecting this prison once and for all, without interference from yourself or anyone. Is that understood?'

'But sir—'

'Do not speak to me. I do not want to hear anything that you have to say. Give them water and wait. I will deal with you afterwards.'

'Hull,' said the doctor, laying a hand on the magistrate's arm, 'really, to remove these men in this fashion during a rescue operation is most cruel. Many of the prisoners have relatives and friends underground. They want to help in finding them. You are interfering in things that you know nothing about.'

'These men appear to require rescuing as much, if not more than those underground. As a medical man, I would expect you to be able to see that for yourself. Now, kindly release me and allow me to do my duty.'

'You are making a mistake.'

'The mistake has already been made, I can see that now.' He put a hand out towards Mrs McBride, saw his filthy nails, his dirty cuff, and withdrew it. 'I am sorry about this,' he said. 'I am very sorry. Of course, meeting tomorrow is now an impossibility for us.' He did not hear what she replied, only saw himself again through her eyes: a man in a suit of mud, with nothing to show for himself but that mud and a yard full of men starving under his care.

There was darkness, and in it water. They dozed above it, wearing the rock like a mantle, their dreams as black as what they woke to. From time to time they spoke one another's names with thick tongues, or allowed a foot to slip into the water, the disturbance lapping long afterwards.

When the light arrived, it was no more than a pinprick, yet it came with an accompaniment of voices that neither man answered. Still, it expanded. A beam, a pool, a wave that carried them out to a world of red, where Noki continued to dream of fetid dust and a sufficiency of rock that no waking could shatter or disperse.

The men stood in ragged lines across the central prison yard. Twenty-five of them, no more than skeletons.

'Are these all the prisoners?' Hull asked of the jailer. He had his hands clasped behind his back and chewed nervously at his moustache.

'Yes, sir.'

'Open the cells.'

'What for? Ain't I telling you this is the lot?'

'By God, I am ordering you. Open the cells.'

Genricks muttered to himself, but he said no more to the magistrate as he limped around the building, unlocking every door that he came to. Hull followed, his hands still gripped behind his back. As each cell was opened, he peered in and saw that they were indeed empty. He nodded at the jailer, but did not look at him. 'Carry on.'

He could already hear the singing of Johnny-boy coming from the last cell on the right-hand side of the passage. The imbecile looked up from a game he was playing, his plump hands holding out a fan of chicken bones. 'Johnny-boy,' he said. The cell was more spacious than the others and contained an iron cot with several blankets folded at the foot end, as well as a riempie chair, and an upturned crate on which treasures had been laid out. Mostly they were bones from various cuts of meat, but Hull recognised amongst the clutter some carved wooden objects similar to those that Genricks had given him and which decorated the mantel in his study.

'I will question this man later. You may lock the door again.'

Genricks did so and turned back towards the prison yard.

'Mr Genricks.' Hull pointed at a narrow door in the corner of the passage, barely noticeable in the shadows. 'You have forgotten to unlock this one.'

'It ain't nought but a closet.'

'For the very last time, Genricks, I am inspecting this jail from top to bottom. You will unlock that door immediately.'

The jailer fiddled with the iron ring in his hands until he located a large rusted key. He inserted it into the lock with some difficulty. Once in, it could not be made to move. 'I told you, sir, it ain't nothing but a closet. We never even use it. Lock's rusted.'

'Step away. Let me try.'

Hull took hold of the key and attempted to twist while at the same time raising the handle and leaning hard against the door with his shoulder. The wood was grey with age, splintering a little under the pressure of the magistrate's arm. At last the key turned with a screech and Hull was able to push the door open.

It was no closet at all. It was a cell, roofless, barely larger than a coffin. There was no sign of a cot or stool nor any type of furnishing or blanket in the place, only a single coloured man, so attenuated that he could barely hold himself up. At his feet the ground was all mire, with not even a paving stone to protect him from the dirt. Though it was the middle of winter, he wore a short pair of breeches and a small jacket with the sleeves cut off. He was no more than skin and bone, yet even so the jacket did not fit across his chest. His ribs, face, arms and legs, every part of him was bruised and scarred. At the door being opened, he had begun to cry silently and collapsed onto the ground.

'What is the meaning of this?'

'It ain't nought, sir. This man is a lunatic.'

'Lunatic or not, he cannot be left like this! Can you not see that he is suffering, that he is very likely dying? He must be put in the hospital at once.'

'Begging your pardon, sir, I know how to deal with lunatics, and Dr Fox—'

'He will be taken to the hospital immediately. Not another word about it. Bring Cloete to me at once.'

The jailer walked to the end of the passage and called for the constable, who entered, following Genricks uneasily.

'Do you know anything about this, Cloete?' Hull asked.

The constable looked inside the cell, turning away at once, a hand to his mouth. 'No sir, I know nothing at all, sir, may God Himself strike me dead. My men and I are not allowed inside the prison, sir. This is my first time to enter it.'

'Not allowed? By whose orders?'

'Company orders, sir. They own the prison.'

'You've not seen the state of the prisoners then?'

'I've seen Johnny-boy, sir.'

'But none of the others?'

'The ones who collect firewood, sir. But none of them looked like this. Not ever, I swear it. This, I've never seen anything like this.'

'Very well. Now, listen carefully, Cloete; I want you to put a guard at the prison door in your stead, then I need you to take this man to the hospital and to find Ned and tell him that I require him to translate for me immediately. Then you come back here. You come inside, do you hear? You come to me. I am ordering you. Forget the Company now. You do as I say, understood?'

'Yes, sir.'

'Nought but a lunatic,' Genricks said again.

'You be quiet. I am going to the yard to interview the prisoners. You will wait outside in the street while I do so.'

'I'll be damned if I do! I'm staying. I ain't letting these bloody devils tell their filthy lies.'

'You will leave. I must insist upon that.'

'I ain't! I'm staying, I tell you. This ain't your prison. You ain't got no power here. You ain't making me leave.'

'I will have you removed if I must.'

'Removed! I'll remove you, that's what I'll do. You'll be the one what is removed!' His face shrunk in on itself with rage, and he raised a fist from his hunched shoulders, advancing on Hull, ready to strike. The magistrate lifted his arm to ward off the blow, but it proved unnecessary. Ned had already arrived, grabbing Genricks by the collar, pulling him back. 'No, Mr Jailer, no.'

'Thank you, Ned. You have come just in time. Please escort this man from the premises. Have him kept outside with the guard until I give permission for him to enter.'

Ned grasped the jailer by his shoulders and pushed him towards the front of the prison.

'You mustn't believe 'em, Mr Hull, sir, they all liars, every last one of 'em. They liars!'

Hull turned his attention to the inmates, who still huddled in the main yard. There was among them no white man. They were dressed much as the prisoner just taken to hospital, in rags that offered little protection from the winter cold, and though they were coated in orange earth from the mines, their emaciation was easily apparent.

'I am the magistrate, Mr Hull,' he said, standing before them, pausing for Ned to translate. 'You need not be afraid. I am asking you to tell me of your treatment in this prison. Genricks is not here; you may speak freely, without any fear.'

What ensued caused him to draw back in surprise. The scene was alarming and unfolded in stages as Ned translated the magistrate's word into several languages. Some of the prisoners flung their hands in the air and began to laugh wildly. Others sank to the ground and wept. A number of them threw themselves at his knees, clasping his legs and shrieking in a way that he might afterwards have described as haunting. It was some minutes before he and Ned were able to return the prisoners to order.

'Please, you are all to be seated,' Hull said, gesturing at the flagstones. 'Now, I would like to hear from each of you in turn. Who would like to begin?'

A middle-aged black man stood with difficulty and spoke in his native language.

'Please, sir,' said Ned, 'he asks if the master would be kind enough to let a pail of water be brought to him.'

Hull nodded, and Cloete moved swiftly from the yard, returning soon with a large basin. 'There was only the slop pail, so I brought this instead, sir.'

'Very well, you may place it in front of him. Ask if that is as he wished, Ned.'

The man removed his jacket and dipped it into the basin. The water instantly muddied. Then he took the wet jacket and used it as a rag to wipe the dirt from his body. He began at his left hand, removing the mud that caked his fingers, palm, wrist and forearm, moving to the elbow and all the way up to his shoulder. He did the same on the other arm. After every swipe of the cloth he returned it to the basin, rinsing it, before bringing it back to his body, where it left streaks of mud as he cleaned. He took time over his belly and chest, washing each inch of skin twice, as by now the water was little more than sludge. Next he removed the small breeches he had been wearing and wiped down his thighs, his calves, his feet. Lastly, he bent down to the basin and splashed water on his face two, three times, wiping the drops off with his hands. He stood naked before the magistrate, displaying his skeletal frame, his jagged limbs and protruding joints, the sickles of his ribs, a face distorted by bruising. His back and extremities were a mass of welts, of yellow ulcers, black crusts. He turned slowly, so that each part of him might be seen, then he gestured at the next man in line to do as he had done, before sitting down, his legs crossed in front of him.

The prisoners came in turn, two of them using the same muddied water before Hull thought to send Cloete and Ned for more. Soon the yard was divided into sections as men bared themselves around decanters, bowls, a porcelain vase. They washed one another, careful over every wound without having to be told, as though they knew the exact placement of each injury as much as if it had been their own. Hull walked among them. They exhibited arms and legs fractured by beatings, breaks that had been left to set crooked. Other than the thrashings, they spoke of old men doused in water and put into bare cells to freeze there all night, of systematic starvation, of their desperate feeding on cockroaches that crawled across the floor and walls. Of the jailer's dull razor, and of being given to Johnny-boy as playthings, afterwards having to watch as the lunatic feasted on the rations of twenty-five men.

'What about the collection of wood? Ask them about that. Genricks told me that he sent them out daily to collect wood. Did nobody see them in this state?'

Several men spoke at once in response to Ned's

question. They pointed. They shook their heads. They clicked their tongues.

'They say that the jailer sends the new prisoners or the white ones, ones that are only in for a few days. Ones he hasn't beaten.'

'I see.'

'But sir, there is more.'

'Yes? Speak, Ned.'

'Sir, they say... they say that many of them have died. They say he has killed them for sport.'

'My God, it is worse than any imagining could have it.'

Towards the back of the yard a man began to cough. Looking up, Hull realised that the prisoners were shivering in the cold evening air, that already the moon was rising and that soon it would be dark. 'Cloete, we must act at once. Choose another constable to assist you, and take these men to the hospital. Give orders that they are to be washed with warm water. Each man is to have a bed and a blanket. Clothes if there are any. Food and drink.'

'Sir, there simply won't be—'

'Do the best that you can. I will come later. Ask at the hotel and pub for cots, by order of the law, make sure that you say that. Mention the Company, if you must. Ask everywhere. There are men and women who can sleep on the floor tonight. There are clothes that others do not need. Go to my house and take my bed, take the linen too. Do what you can.'

'What of Johnny-boy?'

'He can remain here for now. He seems well enough. And Cloete, set a constable to guard the hospital. No one goes in there without permission, least of all Genricks, do you understand?'

'Yes, sir.'

Hull followed the line of men as they made their way outside, observed with disgust the onlookers gaping at their nudity.

From across the street, Genricks shouted, 'What the

hell you done? What you done to 'em? What you done to my men?' At his voice, the prisoners clung to one another, cast about in fright for the magistrate.

'No, Genricks. These are no longer your prisoners,' said Hull, speaking loudly so that all those in the vicinity might hear. 'You may consider yourself under suspension, pending investigation. Constable Cloete is now in charge of the prison, and in addition to that there are constables at the hospital. You are banned from its premises and from these. You will not communicate with the prisoners in any way or form. Now please hand over your keys to my home and to the prison.'

'You ain't doing this!' Genricks yelled, coming forward, trying to enter the building. 'You bastards can go to hell. You ain't doing this to me! I'll see you dead. I'll kill you with me own hands, just you wait.'

But Ned had been standing beside the magistrate and put out a restraining hand, shaking his head. 'Watch your words, Mr Jailer.'

Genricks stumbled backwards, out of reach. 'Don't you touch me, you filth, I'm a cripple. I've a right to my property, a right to what's inside. There's me things in there and I demand 'em be returned to me.'

'Tell me what they are and I will bring them out to you,' said Hull.

Genricks did not reply.

'No? You say nothing? Very well, you leave me little choice.'

Hull entered the office, which was as neat as it had ever been. He opened drawers and ledgers, all the while hearing a thumping sound that may have been the jailer's feet kicking against the wall. In the corner of a shelf, behind three coverless copies of the Bible, Hull found a small bottle with a red label. Upon closer inspection he saw that it read: STRYCHNINE.

He took the bottle into the street and held it up for Genricks to see. 'Where did this come from?'

'I don't know nothing about it.'

'It would be in your interest to remember where this bottle came from.'

'Don't know.'

'Mr Genricks, you have the night to remember the source of this poison. Tomorrow we will discuss it again. Now leave. Leave the vicinity of this building at once and do not consider that returning to it is an option. I have found out the truth about you and you will be punished for it, mark my words.'

The hours of that night were long for Hull, who sat in his study, sleep evading him. He sipped brandy from a cut-glass tumbler that he had no recollection of having purchased, and he wondered how it had come to be here, in this house that he had already begun to hate. He had lit no fire, only a lamp, and he stared gloomily at it now, willing it to go out, for his eyes to be bound by darkness, to fall asleep. The sound of picks on rock could still be heard coming from the mine despite the late hour, and once or twice a call sounded as a discovery was made, but the search had entered its seventh day and the urgency was waning by now, as were the findings. The lamplight flickered slowly and he began to imagine that the flame was moving in time with the beating of the picks, that the fire itself was a pick, tapping away at the glass chimney, hammering to get out. The room shrank until only the flame remained, and he watched its movement, its changing shapes and colours as it hammered. On and on that beating, so loud that it filled the whole room, so immense that it was there with him, very nearly inside him.

Then he started, waking, and the sound continued, coming now from the window. He had not yet drawn the curtains and he was visible to anyone who cared to look in, though he could discern no one from where he sat. He rose and opened the window. It was Genricks, hat in hand, his shoulders hunched higher than ever before. 'Please sir, forgive me for hitting out at you before. I were overcome. You know I'd never harm you, sir. Say you'll forgive me. Can we forget it all, please sir, I beg you.'

'The assault on me is not the subject in question. It is the condition of the prisoners that I cannot ignore.'

'Oh please, sir! Please!' Genricks cried, dropping to his knees, his hands clasped. 'I beg you, don't go on with this investigation. Don't go on with it. You mustn't, sir, you mustn't.'

Hull leaned forward a little, his head just outside the window frame. 'Let me be quite clear with you, Genricks.

I will be sifting this mess to the very bottom. To the very bottom, I tell you. Everything will be revealed.'

'Oh sir, Mr Hull, you ain't hearing me. There's others beside myself what will be in trouble if you do that. You can't do it, see. You'll come to harm.' He was weeping steadily now, his nose running, but he did not lift either hand to wipe it.

'Get up, you coward. Go away from this house and never set foot near it again. Do not speak to me. Do not look at me. You are not welcome here any longer.'

The jailer raised his head to the window and let out a loud, frightening wail as he pulled a pistol from his waistband. 'Ain't I looked after you? Ain't I fed you and washed you? Ain't it me what turned this into a home for you? What was a friend to you when none would have you? Now you turn me away like I'm no more than a piece of dirt. It's all I have in the world and you're taking it from me.'

'You are mistaken, Genricks. I am not your friend and this is not your home. None of this is yours. It never was. I am taking nothing from you. You had nothing and you remain with nothing but your crimes.'

The jailer sobbed. 'You did. You did take it away. You took it all. Where's Genricks' place in the world? Ain't there no place for me?' He lowered the pistol, moving away from the window back into the darkness.

Early the following morning, barely past dawn, Hull went to the prison where he found Cloete on guard. 'Any trouble?'

'Nothing at all, sir. Not a sight or sound of anything.'

'Well, for one of us at least. I want you to find Genricks and arrest him. He came to my home and threatened me. He is armed and I believe his frame of mind to be unstable. Do that and then go home and have a rest. I am certain that you must be exhausted. I am worn out myself.' He held a hand to his brow, breathed out heavily through his nose.

'Yes, sir. Sir?'

'What is it?'

'I wanted to say again, sir, that I didn't know what was happening. Honestly. I would've said something, I swear, I would've.'

'I believe you. It has been a shock to us all. A great shock.'

'Yes, sir. Yes.'

Hull entered the building and unlocked the door to Genricks' office. Someone had closed the shutters, leaving the room in darkness but for a few slats of dim light that showed through the window edges. There was no lamp in the room. Hull went into the passage. The cells had been left open the previous day and he walked past them with care, making sure not to look into them. He was afraid to see the state of them, afraid of what might have been left behind. He removed a lamp from a nail in the wall, and hastened back to the office before lighting it. He took down the ledger books pertaining to the past twelve months, and seated himself at the jailer's desk to study them. For several hours he sat in the quiet, reading every word on the pages. The jailer's writing was surprisingly neat and precise for someone who gave the impression of being uneducated. Hull tore a leaf from the back of one of the ledgers and made notes with a pencil stub that he found lying on the desk. By the time he reached the latest entry, dated a week previously, he had ascertained that in the preceding twelve months, eighteen deaths had been recorded. Three of them in the time that he had been there.

He pushed back the chair, the legs screeching on the flagstones, and went outside, surprised by the daylight. Cloete was gone and another constable was on guard, a man known to him as Witbooi. 'Constable, bring Dr Fox to me, please. I believe he will be at the mine, but you had best send out to Okiep if you cannot find him there as I must see him urgently. I will stand guard while you are gone.'

He waited in the sunlight, face tilted up a little, eyes closed. The day was warm and strangely quiet. Birds sang, and from somewhere nearby he could hear a woman's hum and the splash of water as she washed clothes in a tub. There was no sound to jar the peace of it. He did not think that he had ever experienced the town like this and he began to feel uneasy, certain that something was amiss. He opened his eyes, took in the silent street, then looked across at the mine from where the silence seemed to have emanated and grown, forming now a great weight that was pushing down on the earth. The mine was deserted. The rescue was over.

Fox's voice came, too loud in the quiet. 'What is all this about? I was just sitting down to a pint and I am brought to the prison like a common criminal.'

'Dr Fox, I have some important questions for you. Please come inside so that we might talk in private. Thank you, Witbooi, you may resume your post. No one is to come in or out without my permission.'

'Really, Hull, there's no need to be so serious. We are friends after all. If you want to have a chat then by all means let's have a chat, but don't be so damned dramatic about it. Hasn't there been enough tragedy here these past days?'

Hull led him into the dimly lit office and offered him a chair. 'Have you seen the prisoners that were taken to the hospital yesterday?'

'Of course I have. I'm busy patching them up, aren't I, along with the injured miners.'

'Yet you told me once before that you inspect all prisoners weekly, if not more often.'

'That is correct.'

'You mean to tell me that each week you saw these prisoners and you did nothing to "patch them up", as you describe it, nor did you report their mistreatment at the hands of their jailer?'

'Their injuries are a result of their work in digging out the miners. I have—'

'Nor did you report that in the last year alone eighteen men have died in custody. Eighteen men that you allowed to be interred without any medical examination. Are you aware of the statistics, Dr Fox? In jails of this sort throughout the Cape Colony the average death rate is one person a year for every two jails. Here in a single small town we have had the equivalent number of deaths of thirty-six jails. Within these walls something terrible has been happening and you have been party to it, or at least been aware of it.'

'You have no right—'

'You did not need to examine the men prior to their interment because you knew the cause of their deaths, didn't you?'

'You're going too far now.'

'I must ask you, Dr Fox, I found Genricks in possession of a bottle of strychnine. I have heard from the prisoners that some of those who died did so in convulsions, dying in utter torment. Those are sure signs of poisoning. So, I must ask you, did you supply Genricks with that bottle?'

Dr Fox spoke very quietly. 'Forget all of this, Hull. I am telling you to forget it. Leave it now and all will be all right.'

'Did you supply Genricks with poison? Did you see his prisoners week after week, their bodies weakened by beatings, starvation and poisoning? Did you feel no remorse, no pity when eighteen men were murdered and others very nearly died?'

'Pity? You speak to me of pity? In Paraguay I saw double that number shot before me as I had my morning coffee. Here in the mines we bury easily that number in a month. What does it signify when there are more to be had? I don't value human life like that.' He snapped his fingers. 'It means nothing to me.'

'You will be made to value life if the law has any say in the matter.'

'You have nothing against me, Hull. The Company will stand by me.'

'Are you saying that the Company knows about what has been happening here? That it has had a hand in all this violence?'

Just then Cloete knocked at the door. 'Excuse me, sir, you said I was to let you know. Genricks has been found dead. He shot himself.'

Dr Fox rose to leave. 'You see, Hull. You have nothing against me but your own wild surmisings, and no one to back them up. Good day.'

Hull followed him to the door, watched as he left. 'That man is a monster, I am sure of it. Eighteen lives, Cloete, eighteen lives.'

'Sir, what of Genricks?'

Hull sighed. 'Bring his body here, I suppose.'

'The jackals have been at it, sir.'

'Then bring whatever is left of him. He cannot be left out there like that, no matter his crimes.'

The hospital was little more than a narrow rectangular building with a sparsely thatched roof that had gone to rot in places. It had been built in haste a couple of decades before during a smallpox outbreak. By now the plaster was peeling and many of the window panes were missing, with flour sacks nailed up in their stead to keep out the light and cold. An array of cots and wooden beds lined the walls, interspersed with straw mattresses or reed mats on which convicts and miners lay together. Initially an attempt had been made to keep whites and natives separate, but as the injured flowed out of the ground, they were placed wherever a spot was available. Men coughed, spat. They urinated where they lay, their open wounds attracting flies. All about lingered the odour of rotting flesh, the crisp sweetness of carbolic acid.

There had only ever been one nurse employed at the hospital, Matron Gladwell, a widow whose husband had been an engineer at the mine in the early days. He had died several years before, and she, well into her sixties, had not seen the purpose in leaving the village she had known for 30 years. In times of trouble, like the plagues of influenza or flux, she commandeered local housewives and girls to assist her, but otherwise she ran the hospital alone.

'So you have come at last, Mr Hull,' she called across the ward as he entered. 'A fine thing to set upon me in that way yesterday evening when we are already in a crisis. Twenty-five beds to be found, and instructions that the men be washed and fed. Very nice, indeed. How, I ask you? There's hardly room for a mouse to turn over in its sleep, let alone all the other things you demand.'

'Yes, I can see that, Mrs Gladwell. You are doing admirably considering your difficulties.'

'I should say so. And yet all the while my every movement is being watched. Really, Mr Hull, in all my years as matron of this hospital it has never been deemed necessary for me to be under a constable's constant observation.'

'My dear lady, the constable, I assure you, is here only for the prisoners.'

'Well, he's a useless lout as it is. Keeps nodding off. I'm forever having to shout at him to wake up. You would have a better guard in a plank of wood.'

Hull called the constable over from where he had been leaning in the doorway. He was a Baster man, very small and dark, with the green irises that many of that tribe boasted. Yet fatigue had threaded his eyes with red, and he yawned as he approached.

'How long have you been on duty, Smallie?'

'All night and all of today so far. There's no one to relieve me, sir.'

'That will not do. Send for my clerk, Jakob. He can stand duty for you for a few hours while you eat and rest. Then you are to find my two assistants, Ned and Oupa. Tell them to go first to the stables and get a horse and cart. Then they must go to the store here and afterwards to the one in Okiep. Tell them to bring back every blanket, every pair of trousers, every shirt. Socks, too, if they are to be had. Then you tell them to bring two sheep, and vegetables – potatoes, pumpkins, whatever can be found – all of it on my account, you understand. Here's a note for the stableman and one for the store-keeps. Do you have all that? Do you need me to repeat it?'

'No, sir. I have it, sir.'

Hull turned to the matron and bowed a little as he spoke. 'I hope that you will find this of some assistance. The patients must be kept warm. At all times each patient must be warm and fed. They are not to go hungry under any circumstances.'

'Thank you, Mr Hull. You are very good to send for those things, and they will be of great help, but I believe I know my job well enough without the need for further interference. Once your men return, I will have a broth made for all the patients. The prisoners in particular must be fed with care. It cannot be too rich at first or they will

153

become ill.'

'Very well, I leave it in your hands, Mrs Gladwell. There are men here close to death, I fear. They must be made to live.'

She nodded and surveyed the ward, before shouting towards the far end of the room, 'Not like that, you foolish girl. Lift him up, lift him up when you do that.'

Noki lay on his side, facing the sack wall of the hut. Though it was cold, he wore nothing. Since late morning he had lain like this, and now, with darkness rising, fires were being lit throughout the settlement as people prepared for the night. But Noki made no movement, staring only as the sacking bruised into blackness, from time to time letting through a small pinprick of light. There was the sound of crackling wood, of voices, and then again that pinprick, causing him to close his eyes and see it no more.

After being rescued, he had been told to go home; the hospital was full. Yet Noki had found the walk home impossible to make. Not out of exhaustion or weakness, but because of the number of empty shacks he would have had to pass, with no more at the end of them than his own empty hut. The pathway through the settlement seemed to him like a dark tunnel, the hut itself like the small space in which he and Tregowning had been trapped for all those days. He felt no thirst, no hunger, only sorrow and loneliness. In his desperation he had sought out Moses, forgetting that he was dead until he saw the mournful eyes of the boy. He stammered his regrets, tried to speak of what he recalled only dimly, the hours before the collapse. Solomon listened without expression, bringing afterwards a bowl of pap, and water so that Noki might wash his face and hands. And when Noki fell asleep on the floor of the hut, he did not wake him, did not beg to be left alone with his grief.

At daylight he gave Noki a cup of hot water infused with bitter leaves from the veld. 'There's no more coffee.'

Noki nodded, sipped as he felt for sleep around his eyes.

'I did not tell you yesterday because you were tired...' the boy said.

'What?'

'The prisoners. They've been released. They're all in the hospital.'

He threw down the tin cup, ran, bare feet plat-platting

155

on the ground. Solomon followed behind.

At the entrance to the hospital, Constable Smallie held out his arm and stopped them from going further. He surveyed Noki's cut head, his hands and feet, his torn lips. 'Not injured enough. We're full up, sorry.'

'I'm looking for someone.'

'So's everyone. I can't let anyone in. There's an inquiry.'

'I only want to know if my brother is well. He's a prisoner.'

'If he's in here then he's in a bad state, I'll tell you that much. If he isn't... then it's worse.'

'And you can't find out for me? You can't tell me if he is in there?'

Smallie began to shake his head.

Solomon said, 'We give you the name. It's easy. Just a name and you say yes or no.'

'Listen, all prisoners were in for minor offences. The magistrate has pardoned them all, unconditionally. They're free to go as soon as they're healthy enough. So just have some patience. That's all I can tell you. If your brother is in here, he'll be out soon.'

They moved away, Solomon saying 'This way,' and pulling him around the corner to the back of the building. Women, children and men from the settlement had gathered there while two boys held up a sash window, relaying news. Noki waved his hand at the boys, called, 'Hey, hey! Ask for Anele Noki, a prisoner. I'll give you a shilling.'

A shiver went through the crowd. A shilling was a lot of money.

Noki waited, saw lips shape his brother's name, whispers following, and soon one of them was turning back towards him, 'He's not here. He's dead.' Then he and the other boy were jumping from the sill and Matron was yelling, 'Get away there. Give these men some peace, for heaven's sake!' She slammed the window shut.

The crowd began to disperse, muttering to one another

that they would return later, that they would make other attempts to communicate with those inside. Noki remained, his eyes on the closed window until a hand was held out towards him. It was the boy who had spoken so lightly, who had said *dead* as though it were nothing at all. He reached into his pocket, found the coin, placed it in the open palm. The boy smiled, moved off, laughing with his friend.

Solomon began to speak, but Noki shook his head, 'Not now.' He walked through the paths he had previously dreaded entering. He saw nothing on either side of him, as though they were indeed those underground passages he had feared, walled in by an endlessness of rock and rock and rock. When he reached his shack, he stripped off his dirty clothes and lay down. With one hand he traced the scars on his shoulders and back, feeling the welts left from five years on the mines. Inside each scar lived an orange tint where the dirt had buried itself inside him.

Hull was not able to return to the hospital until the following day. He went through the ward, checking that everyone was comfortable, that blankets and clothing had been shared equally. He gave out plugs of tobacco and packs of playing cards to those well enough to sit up for a game. Next he went outside through the back door of the building to where a makeshift kitchen had been erected in order to cater for the increased number of patients. A large potjie stood over a fire. Two women were chopping vegetables and chattering to one another. Hull lifted the heavy lid with a stick and peered through the steam to see a sheep's head bubbling in broth. Meat was falling from the skull, revealing the sharp bones of the snout. 'Have you enough of everything?'

'At the moment, yes.'

He began to say that they were to advise him as soon as they needed anything further, but was interrupted by the entrance of a Hottentot whom he recognised as a servant of the Super. The man was carrying a large wooden crate full of jars. Mrs McBride followed, holding a heavy basket. Hull took it from her, stammering, 'Oh, good morning.'

'Why, Mr Hull,' she smiled, 'I didn't think to see you here.'

'Nor I you.'

'There is a great deal of dissatisfaction in sitting at home and doing nothing. I cannot accept it as easily as others might. I must be of some use. I must do what I can, as you are. In fact, it was you who inspired me to come here today.'

'How so?'

'I watched your men from the window yesterday and saw them going into the store. It was clear to me that there was a terrible need as they quite emptied the shelves. I resolved to come here and do some good if I was able.'

'I am surprised that your father allowed you to travel all this way on your own.'

'Father is not here, and he need not know about it. He

has gone to Cape Town in order to convince investors to reopen the Blue Mine now that the rescue is over.'

'Oh.'

She reached over to the basket and took out a jar. 'I have brought some marmalade and other jams for the patients. We had such an abundance of fruit that came with the ship.'

'You made this?'

'Oh, not on my own. We all helped. We sat out on the back porch cutting the fruit, even Father helped before he left. In fact, were it not for the great tragedy surrounding us at present, it might have been a moment from my early childhood, when we still lived in the Cape in a large farmhouse, and where we were quite happy for a short time.' She handed the jar to him. 'But then, of course, I found that it was not right to eat these luxuries, not after what I had seen on the mine the other day, and not after your men coming to the store.'

'But your father can eat such things? He is happy to order fruit and pheasants and whatever else he desires while there are men starving under his care?'

Mrs McBride frowned. 'I don't understand, Mr Hull. What is it that you are saying? The jail is not in the care of my father. It is in your care, is it not?'

'Is that what you think of me? That I torture men for my own pleasure? That I starve them to death and beat them and poison them?'

'No. Of course not. How could I think that? What has made you so angry?'

'I am angry because I have seen, with great clarity and far too late, what a fool I have been. All of this. I have allowed all of this to happen,' he gestured at the hospital, the makeshift kitchen, the pot on the fire.

'Do you mean the prisoners? Surely you cannot be to blame for what they have suffered? Surely it has been some dreadful error, a mistake.'

'Please, Mrs McBride,' he said, shaking his head,

'just recently you spoke to me of how useless subtlety and excuses are. I must take your example and speak with frankness. You cannot be here; you must leave.'

'Whatever for? What have I done?'

'Please,' he said, returning the jar to the basket and pointing at the crate. 'Take these. There will be an investigation. If any of the prisoners should die having eaten—'

'Die! What on earth are you saying?'

'Please go, I beg you. Take it all and do not bring anything else. You must leave at once. For God's sake, stay away.'

He did not return to the jail that day, nor did he go to the Residency. Instead he went to the pub and sat at a table, calling to Alfred for a double brandy. The place was nearly empty. Only a few men stood at the bar, and two others sat together at a table. He drank down his first glass, then ordered another. After a while the two men at the table left, and Hull called again for Alfred. When he ordered the fourth drink, a coloured girl sidled up to him and sat on his lap, holding the glass to his lips.

Later, when all was dark, when his eyes had stopped seeing, his mouth stopped tasting, he allowed himself to be led into a small dark room at the back of the building. He lay down on a reed mat and thought of nothing as the naked woman sat astride him, speaking words he could not hear.

In the morning Noki woke to the sound of a Baster man calling his name and opening the flap of his hut. 'God, it stinks in here,' said the man. 'Hurry up, you filth. Waterboer wants to see you.'

'I'm not interested in seeing him.'

'You're forcing me to come inside, are you? You're forcing me to come inside this stink.' He held his nose closed with one hand and with the other pulled Noki up off the mat on which he lay. 'Get dressed. Waterboer's waiting.'

Noki put on the same clothes that he had worn for all of his days underground. They were reeking, stiff with dirt, but he had no others. The man led him out of the settlement, across no man's land to the Village.

Waterboer met Noki in his tent, a Bible open in front of him as it had been the last time. The Griqua chief smiled, stood up from his campaign chair and walked across the tent with an outstretched hand. 'Molefi, I am glad to see that God has seen fit to save you from death. There are many that He did not. So many of our fellow miners have suffered with the collapse of the Blue Mine.'

Noki shook the proffered hand, feeling how soft and plump it was. That hand had never laboured.

'Some time ago you came here accusing me of being responsible for your brother's imprisonment. I am sorry to have to tell you that I have been informed that your brother is dead.'

'I know.'

'In his case it was not God who took him, but rather a servant of Satan in the form of that Genricks demon. He murdered your brother and many men from my tribe too. Those he did not kill lie close to death in the hospital. I have been praying for them.'

He moved around the tent, gesturing with his plump forefinger as he spoke. 'Unfortunately, the demon has chosen suicide rather than face God for his actions. But he will be punished. He will live in hell for all eternity for what he has done. God has promised it and I pass that message on to you that you may be comforted.'

'How will that comfort me?'

'Ah, my heathen friend, because hell is a pit, deep down in the bowels of the earth, a pit of terrible heat, each breath like fire, with the promise of agonising pain. His body will be broken and aching.'

'That is what you call hell?' Noki clicked his tongue in irritation. 'Why did you call me here?'

'My young friend, if you had only taken the time to make space in your heart for the Lord then you would know that He teaches us to love all creatures. I extend my hand to you. You loved your brother; he was murdered. I loved my men; they were murdered. I invite you to come with me to the magistrate.'

'What for?'

'Even I know that there are times when God's justice is not enough.' He called a few words in Dutch, and the guard who had brought Noki to the Village entered, accompanied by a man dressed in a brand-new wool suit that hung from his emaciated frame. Around his neck an elaborate and large cravat, crimson with white polka-dots, had been tied, most likely by hands other than his own.

'Now we are all here, so if you would...' Waterboer said, motioning towards the tent entrance. Noki followed behind the guard and the thin man as they left, but soon he was walking beside them, so that the four men spread across the pathways of the Village. Inhabitants made way, women curtsied at their Kaptijn, men doffed a hat if they had one, bowed their heads. Waterboer blessed those he passed, walking with his right hand raised above his shoulder, as though swearing an oath.

At first glance, Noki had taken the thin man for an ancient of the tribe, someone long since meant for the grave, but walking beside him now, he recognised that the furrows and dried-out skin were due to malnourishment, not age. The man could not have been more than 30 years old. He walked stiffly, his legs, hobbled by starvation, jerking painfully under the swathes of clean cloth, with that ridiculous cravat jumping up towards his chin, threatening to engulf his face.

Constable Witbooi was on duty. 'Please, Kaptijn,' he said, 'the magistrate is not to be disturbed. That's what he told me: not to be disturbed. But, my Kaptijn, if you let me know your business and wait here, I will go and announce you and see if he will talk with you.'

'Announce me? Is that how you address your Kaptijn, Wynand Witbooi?'

'No, sir. But the magistrate—'

'This is God's business. It needs no announcement. Step aside, please.'

Witbooi moved away from the doorway, pressing himself against the wall as Waterboer passed. The three others followed him into the office, finding the magistrate behind the desk, making notes.

Hull looked up, surprised. 'I am very busy at this moment. I am afraid I can see no one just now. I must ask you to leave. My constable should have stopped you. I will have to have a word with him.'

'No word is necessary,' Waterboer smiled. 'Witbooi knows the true Word. The Word of God. That is why he has allowed us to enter and that is why we cannot leave now, Mr Hull. We have come to speak with you. Perhaps you know who I am?'

Hull shook his head.

'It is a pity that we have not been introduced before. Your predecessor knew me well. My name is Waterboer and I am, much like yourself, an important man here. I am leader of the Griqua people of Springbokfontein. Now you see why I must insist on speaking to you.'

'Indeed, I do not.'

'I have come because our tribe has been struck down by pestilence as foul as the plagues of Egypt. Our people have died and may still be dying. That is why God has sent me to you, to tell you that first we lost our people in the mine and then we discovered that our men, in your own prison, have been murdered and tortured.'

Hull stood up. 'There is not yet any proof of murder.

165

You cannot speak of murder.'

'Murder is the only word I know for what has happened.'

'Mr Waterboer, I am doing my utmost, I assure you, to investigate this matter thoroughly.'

'And what is your investigation to us? At least when the Company murders our men in the mines they pay some compensation. It is a trifle only, but it is something. Yet when they kill the prisoners we are offered nothing.'

'The Company is no longer in charge of this prison. I am.'

'Then it is you who must pay us in order to appease God for the atrocities that have been committed within these walls.'

Noki stepped forward. 'Waterboer, you spoke to me of justice. Is money the justice that you say is higher than God? If it is then I want no part of it.' He turned towards Hull. 'What I want is for my brother to be returned to me, Mr Magistrate. If I cannot have him alive then at least I want his body. There are bodies in the mine now, buried where no one can find them. I don't want the same thing for my brother.'

'Yes,' said Waterboer, adding quickly, 'we want their bodies and you must pay for their funerals.'

'Mr Waterboer, you are going too fast. There are no bodies. Genricks is dead. I can get no word of sense from Johnny-boy. How am I to know where or even how Genricks disposed of the bodies? Believe me, you are not the only ones who want them. I need them for my inquiry.'

Waterboer put his arm around the narrow shoulders of the thin man, pushing him forward. 'This is Pieter Klaasen. Until two days ago he was a prisoner in your jail.'

'He should still be in hospital. He is in no fit state to be walking about. Who released him?'

Waterboer ignored the question. 'Pieter was in this jail for six months. During that time Genricks took him out eight times at night and made him dig graves. He can show us where the bodies are.'

166

They went slowly through the streets of Springbokfontein and the eerie stillness of the Blue Mine. Beyond, they passed the cemetery with its pale grey headstones. It was close to full already, so that soon the white community would need to move the stone wall, extend its reach. Graves marked the lives of several babies and children, of wives felled by childbirth and men struck down by the mine in various ways. Against the far wall a couple of the gravestones had fallen over. No one had bothered to re-erect them. Those who might remember the deceased were long since dead themselves, or else had left the region for some kinder place.

The incline was steep, and more than once Pieter seemed likely to collapse. Waterboer's guard assisted him, held him upright until they reached the summit. A plateau of sorts spanned to the right. Pieter pointed to a koppie of red sand and boulders at the far end of the plateau, speaking quietly to Waterboer. 'He says we will find the graves there. He says that when he could, he placed a stone or twigs as a marker. But for now you can see that he is tired. Let us go ourselves while he rests a moment. Afterwards he will take us to the other sites.'

'Other?' said Hull.

'There are three.'

Noki held up three fingers to Pieter in query.

The man nodded, then spoke, this time with more animation, lifting his thin arms to point first at the koppie, then across to another one some 800 feet away. Finally, he gestured across the valley to a koppie on the far side of the town.

'He says Genricks used all three sites simultaneously so that no single one became full too quickly or was in danger of being discovered.'

'He was a fiend,' said Hull.

'Pieter tells me that the sites have names,' continued Waterboer, 'but whether they were named by Genricks or by the prisoners themselves, he cannot say. This one here is Duiwelskop, that one is Niehoop and the far one is Huisverlaaten. I will translate for you, Mr Hull. They are dreadful names in their way. Devil's Head, No Hope and Leaving Home.' He paused and wiped his brow. His eyes were damp. 'I know that it was I who sought to bring you here, but now I find I cannot go closer. Satan is strong in this place and I am weak with grief. You go, you two, please.'

Noki and Hull scaled Duiwelskop quickly. If there had once been grave markings, they were now impossible to see. The entire koppie was scattered with stones and bushes, as was the surrounding region.

'It's all gone,' said Noki. 'There is no way to find them like this.'

'No, we cannot allow this to be the end. We cannot be put off. I will have this entire koppie dug up. I will see it destroyed. Every single body will be exhumed. There will be nothing left of this cursed hill.'

Noki scanned the dirt, swatted a fly from his face. 'I'll help you. I'll dig for them.'

Eight further men volunteered, all of them tribal. No white man stepped forward. Hull separated them into three groups and delegated a hillock to each. Noki was on the Duiwelskop team with Tengo and a Baster man known as Jong Thys. They dug in rows, ploughing up the hill side by side. Rains had left the first metre of soil partially wet, making it easy to slide out with spades, but soon they were shifting through loose sand that parted and met in inconvenient waves.

From time to time Noki paused and stared across at the other koppies. At Huisverlaaten he could make out two men lifting something from the earth. If it was a rock they would roll it down, he thought. If it was a rock they would not take such care in carrying it. He looked away. On the cart-track below, twelve men were walking with spades. They climbed over the low wall of loose stones that bounded the cemetery and sauntered between the headstones until they came to an empty row, squashed between two others, the area thick with weeds. Their voices were faint in the still air. One of them brought out a ball of string and they began to mark off spaces. Noki waited as two graves were evenly measured out, knowing there were many more to follow.

Behind him Tengo said quietly, 'I think I have one' and Noki went to where he knelt.

He had uncovered part of a torso. It was desiccated, preserved by the dry sand so that no decay had occurred. Noki scraped with his hands, uncovering a shoulder, a neck, a face. The head was twisted upwards, the skin pulled tight over the skull. Several teeth were missing. The lower jaw was broken. He worked slowly until he was able to draw the body from the earth. He held it on his lap, those angular limbs, that disfigured face that had once belonged to his brother.

They came with the corpses blinkering them, one on each shoulder. There was no weight to the bodies. Still, they were carried with some difficulty, the view made narrow, so that each man saw only the footprints of the previous one ahead of him, and slumped through the troubled sand towards the cottage at the far end of the Residency grounds. The entrance was low, forcing them to bend a little, lower their heads. Most shifted one of the bodies to under an arm, or left the other beside the stone step as they went indoors. There were more bodies than they could carry in one trip, and so they returned to the sites, taking a moment to wipe their brows with freed hands, or to make adjustments to their clothing. Those who came last had asked for sacks, and they brought the remains in these, the contents rattling loosely as they walked.

Hull stood a little way from the cottage, as though the distance might excuse him of what was inside. He did not enter.

Later, once night had fallen, he lit a lamp and walked out into the gloom behind the Residency. Nearing the cottage, he saw the yellow glow of a pair of eyes low to the ground. He picked up a stone, threw it, shouted. The eyes disappeared. Yet he felt them on him still as he unlocked the cottage, and he entered hastily, shutting the door with a bang, bolting it from the inside. The lamp cast his shadow large against the wall. It flickered above the rows of corpses, a black thing that made the uneven stones come to life.

He leaned against the door, breathing shallowly through his mouth, afraid of what he might smell. After several minutes he willed himself to sit down at a small desk that Ned had brought in earlier. He wrote numbers onto brown cardboard tags. Next he approached the bodies, tying a label to each one. He recorded the positions in which they lay, their height, number of teeth, and examined them for signs of brutality – perforations in the skin, broken ribs, fractured bones.

170

From time to time he returned to the small table to dip his pen in the inkpot. On one occasion he paused, hearing scratching at the cottage door. 'Hello?' he called, but did not open it. 'Hello?' Later he heard growls, a yelp, more scratching. All night, the outsiders tried to get in.

Late morning, Hull dressed in a black suit and went out into the main street of the town. There were others too, if not in black then in their Sunday best. All of them went in the same direction, many slowed by limps and broken bones. He observed Tregowning some way ahead of him, wearing a jacket through one arm, the other hanging loosely over a bandaged shoulder. He had wet his hair, and was smoothing it down flat, hat in hand, as he walked.

'Jory,' Hull called and trotted over. 'I heard you had been rescued. I had meant to come see you. We parted on bad terms before and I am sorry for that. But I am happy to see that you are well. Have you been discharged?'

'This morning. The matron said I had ants in my pants and I was disturbing the other patients,' he laughed. 'Besides, there's not much more they can do for me. I just have to wait for this damn arm to heal.'

'Are you attending the funeral?'

He nodded. 'Do you think the Super will be there? He has not shown his face throughout any of this.'

'He's still in the Cape, last I heard.'

They entered the graveyard and joined the sixty or so other mourners who had assembled at the freshly dug graves. Amongst them were Dr Fox and Mrs Townsend, along with Katrina and Mrs McBride. She wore her veil again, and though Hull noticed her head turning in his direction, she gave no indication of having seen him. Katrina's dress was inconsiderately garish, her hairstyle more suited to a ball than a funeral. She frowned, seemingly displeased by the ramshackle fashions of those around her, and leaned close to her sister, whispering something in her ear. Mrs McBride folded her hands in front of her, shook her head a little.

The service began with a prayer from the priest. Tregowning clucked his tongue. 'Most of these men were Methodists. Why is the Anglican priest giving the service?'

A man in front of them turned and said, 'Use your head, mate. The Methodist pastor is an NCC man. He wouldn't be

172

at a CCMC funeral.'

'Not even in a case like this, when the deaths have been so tragic?' Hull asked.

The man shrugged. 'Company's in charge.'

The service was monotonous, the hymns tedious in their length. Eventually the final amen was spoken, and the priest announced that a collection would be taken up for the widows and children of the deceased. A deep wooden bowl was passed around the assembled. When it reached Tregowning, he handed it straight on.

'You will give nothing?' Hull asked, putting a handful of coins in the plate.

'No. These were good men and I am sorry for their deaths. But there were many equally good men that died too and we are not standing at their gravesides.'

'There will be no such funeral for the natives then?'

'If there is it will not be at Company expense. Besides, many families have already taken the bodies back home to have traditional burials. There's nothing to keep them here now without a man to earn a living.'

'But the women and children can still work, surely?'

'Yes, some will stay, but they are unlikely to earn enough to live on. I want to help them somehow. I've a little money saved up. It's not much, but it's enough to do something for a few, for a short while at least.'

'Please, I would like to contribute. Here,' he felt in his pockets and handed over what he had. 'I have more at the Residency. I will bring it to you later.'

'That is decent of you.'

'How can I not be decent after I have been earning money for a job that I did not do? It would not be honest to keep it. Men were murdered and starved because I was blind to it: I cannot allow any more people to go hungry, no matter the reason.'

The mourners began to disperse slowly, though Fox was in haste and pushed past Hull and Tregowning, bumping the magistrate's shoulder with some roughness.

'How do things stand with him?' Tregowning asked, as they watched the man stride down the hill.

'He's a criminal as far as I am concerned. He had to have been involved in those deaths somehow, but I have no proof as yet.'

Mrs Townsend and Katrina came next, nodding coldly. Last was Mrs McBride. She made a show of ignoring Hull, but when a few feet away, turned back. 'I once thought you something separate, Mr Hull, something good in this dreadful place. But you have shown yourself to be otherwise; Dr Fox informs me that you will be investigating himself and my father. In your mind we are all murderers and poisoners.'

'Not so, Mrs McBride, but I must do my duty, even at the risk of offending those I care about.'

'Your duty? Do you not know that you are an object of ridicule? You rush through your cases so that you can roam around the countryside in search of your precious specimens. Well, you have them now. A whole cottage of specimens for you to study and delight in. What a fine man you are, playing at justice when all the while you are no more than a child in a sand pit.' She walked away to where her mother and sister waited. She did not look back.

Hull reached up and removed his hat, pressed his fingers to his brow. He knew what he was, knew the farce of himself. Still, it did not lessen the pain of hearing Mrs McBride's words against him, spoken with such undisguised loathing.

He went slowly from the cemetery, observing nothing in his descent back into town, but a door slamming somewhere startled him into looking up, and he saw as though with new eyes what he had lived in and grown accustomed to these past months. The dull sky, the wearying streets and stained homes, the disgrace of the prison building, Smallie asleep on the step, the Residency with its monstrous furniture, and the futile Magistracy beside it. How many years had it been this way? How long had the town, and others around it, toiled and suffered, toiled and suffered under the Company's command? No individual could ever hope to alter or redeem it.

Even so, he continued towards the hospital, stopping only to nod grimly at Witbooi before entering. There could be no giving up. There could not be, though determination meant very little in the face of all he had seen.

Matron Gladwell led him to where four prisoners lay together on a pile of blankets. Their heads had been shaved and they wore clean clothes of varying styles. 'These men are well enough to be interviewed, and I believe they all speak English. But mind, no more than fifteen minutes, Mr Hull. Do you understand?'

'Yes, thank you, Matron. I will do my best not to distress them.'

He sat down on a three-legged stool beside the men, took a notebook and pencil from his jacket pocket. 'Good afternoon. Good afternoon. I hope that each one of you is beginning to feel a return of strength and health. I am busy with my investigation into the manner of the deaths of those prisoners who died in custody and I was hoping that some of you might be able to recollect anything that might be useful.'

The men looked back at Hull with blank faces, and he cleared his throat. 'I am certain it is not easy or pleasant to do, but I would be grateful if you could.'

A young man with a woman's shawl draped around his shoulders said, 'I can remember that Klaas was beaten with a broom handle. I remember that, and we had to pick bits of his skull off the ground.'

'And when was that? Can you recall?'

'Maybe two weeks ago, I think. Or maybe three. Or four, I'm not sure now.'

The man to his left was wearing an unmatched pair of socks, the only one among them to have anything on his feet. 'That's right, it was a broom for Klaas, and Gezwindt died when Johnny-boy sat on his chest and held him while

175

Genricks sliced off his nostrils and lips. Do you remember that?'

'No, that was Jan Boom,' said a middle-aged man with a bruised cheek healing to yellow. 'I remember Jan Boom screaming.'

'I remember Gezwindt screaming.'

'Which one did he haul up to the ceiling on a pulley and then drop on his head?' asked the fourth man.

'I wasn't there then. That must have been before me,' said the man with the socks.

'It was two men,' answered the bruised man. 'Two men in one week. One of them was a Herero. I don't know his name. The other was an old Xhosa man. We called him Deputy.'

'No, you're not remembering properly. Deputy was beaten to death with a chair leg,' said the man in the shawl.

'No, that was Links Abraham. He was beaten and then his face held in the sand until he suffocated.'

'I remember,' said the man with the socks.

'You weren't there.'

'But I remember. I remember. I can't forget. I remember.'

They did not ask for more than what they believed was owed to them – the right to identify their dead. Ned made them line up outside, letting them in one at a time. Hull followed with his notebook and pencil. 'No touching,' he said more than once, moving the bodies himself if necessary.

The first to enter was a Zulu woman with a baby tied to her back. She went through each of the cottage's three rooms, returned to the second, but after looking one more time, shook her head. She kept her gaze away from the pile that had been stacked in a corner, away from the two skulls, the numerous ribs and other bones. No, she said, her husband was not there.

Next came an old Griqua woman, accompanied by Waterboer, his hair perfumed with oil, and loose around his shoulders. They found her son in what had once been the cottage's kitchen and knelt beside him. Waterboer prayed, the woman keened. At the end of the prayer, she clasped her hands together, begged that she be allowed to stay beside her boy. But Hull spoke quietly in response to the Kaptijn's request, 'It's not possible today. I'm sorry. Others are waiting their turn. I'm very sorry.' Waterboer nodded and gently lifted the woman by her arms, helping her to the doorway, her mournful wailing locking itself to the room, the cottage, the bodies inside.

So it went throughout the hours of daylight. Some found their dead, others did not. Many were uncertain, pointing at several corpses as possibilities. A number of times different families laid claim to the same body. Hull made no comment. He wrote down what they told him, adding diagrams as required. Only afterwards, when the room was again still and he tried to make sense of his notations, did he see the horrible futility of it. Words on pages. Names and names and names. And all around him, bodies. How could he bring them together with any certainty?

Next, idleness came for most. They loafed in the settlement, the pub, the hospital. They wandered the streets, visited the ruined mine where Reid sat with his feet up and a hat over his face, shrugging them away with, 'Damned if I know a thing, boys. I'm waiting for word just the same as you.'

Hunger and boredom drove Noki and Solomon into the veld where they set traps. But others had preceded them, and still more followed, so that they caught nothing. Instead, they took to traipsing long distances into the wilderness, sleeping out at night. They fashioned spears for themselves and knobkieries, the weapons of their ancestors, and taught themselves how to use them when hunting. In the evenings they lay wrapped in skin blankets, eating their kill around a small fire.

'Ah, this is good,' Noki said.

'The meat?'

He laughed. 'Yes, the meat, and all of this. The sky and those stars there and the earth here all around us, with not a mine in sight. Just us and the earth, and we don't have to enter it. We can just lie here and be at peace.'

'Do you think you won't go back to the mine then?'

'I don't know. We don't even know if it will re-open. Maybe I'll just go home, be with Lulama, work my land. That mine... I don't know. I don't want to think about it. And what about you? Will you go home to your mother and your sisters?'

'I have to stay here. It's my duty to earn money and to send it back to them. We have no one else to depend on. It has to be me.'

Noki sighed. 'Yes. I know. Yes.' He spoke again after a moment, trying to make his voice lighter than he felt. 'Well, I can have a word with the Cousin Jack, if you want. See if he'll take you on in your father's place. We can work together, you and me and Tengo. It'll be good.'

The boy nodded, then spoke softly. 'You told me before that he did a lot for my father that day.'

'Who? The Cousin Jack? He did. He did a lot. As much

as he could.'

'But not enough.'

Noki raised himself on his elbow. 'What are you saying? You can't blame him for your father's death?'

'Why not when he's alive and my father's dead?'

'I'm alive too, Solomon. Am I to blame as well, is that what you think?'

'I don't think anything. I only...' He sat up. 'Look, it's easy for you. You have Genricks to hate and to blame. Who can I blame? Don't say the Company. What is the Company? I want a face, there must be a face. Someone who comes and stands right here in front of me and says, "I did it. I killed your father. It was me."'

'And what then?'

'Then I'll kill him.'

Noki sat up now too, throwing the skin from around his shoulders. 'Solomon, do you hear yourself? You've been spending too much time with Zamikhaya, that's what's making you speak like this. Don't say you'll kill people. You're a good boy, you're not this person.'

'Aren't I? Don't you believe you can be forced to violence when everything else, every other option is taken away from you? Don't you believe in that?'

'Listen to me, so many people have died already. What can it solve? Really, Solomon, what can it solve?'

'So, you'll do nothing about what happened to Anele?'

'Of course I'm doing something. The magistrate—'

'Don't talk to me about the magistrate. He's nothing to you or me. I want to know what can we do, us, us, what can we do? That's the thing that I ask myself every night, every day. What can these hands do?'

It came when they had begun to lose hope that it ever would: the call to assemble at the mine. The mood was light at the news, the whole town seeming to rise from a long-held breath. They walked in excitement, levity issuing from them without restraint. The mine would reopen, that was it. It would reopen and they would work again.

As they approached the old pithead, they saw that a small mound had been raised for the purpose of an announcement. Spades still leant against its base, and several men stood sweating nearby. Reid climbed the low heap and addressed the gathered faces. 'Right you lot, the Super has sent word. London and Cape Town say we reopen the Blue Mine.'

Cheers followed, some throwing hats in the air, embracing, grabbing hold of one another and saying, 'I told you, didn't I? Didn't I tell you it would happen?' Men joked, kissed their wives and children, spoke of money to come, with promises of new clothes, of meat and cake, of things being better this time round, just you wait and see, by God, they'd be better!

Reid motioned for silence. 'Listen, listen, it's only going to be repair work, all right. Clearing it out, making it workable again. We're talking six months, a year. No sorters, no women and children. No tut and tribute work. No skilled and unskilled. Whites get a flat rate of one shilling six per day and the rest of you get four pence a day. That's it.'

For a moment the crowd was silent. Then, 'You can't be serious,' called a man and 'It's not fair, it's not possible,' said others.

'Come on, Reid,' said a Swedish man known as Red Sven, 'this must be a joke.'

'Look,' said the mine boss, 'those are the rates I've been told and it's the only way this mine can stay open. Work or don't work. Those are your choices. If you want to eat then you report to work tomorrow as usual.'

He began to step down from the mound, but paused

when Tregowning shouted out to him from the back of the crowd, 'What about safety?'

'What about it?'

'Will you give us more supports? The props we should have had in the first place?'

'You'll have the same number as before. The Company believes that number to be sufficient.'

'You mean cheap enough!' yelled Red Sven.

Others agreed with him, and the discontent persisted, voiced from all sides.

'You want to kill us? You killed off half the miners and now you want to kill the rest,' shouted a white man with a bandaged temple.

'We can't work like that, you stingy bastard,' shouted Zamikhaya, and 'It's slavery is what it is,' said another.

By now Tregowning had come forward. He raised his bandaged arm as far as he could. 'You can't really expect us, any of us, to work in dangerous conditions without suitable equipment, and then you pay us less for risking our lives. It's not even enough to feed a man, let alone his family.'

'You can be grateful the mine's reopening,' said Reid. 'There was talk of closing it down altogether and then you lot would be out of a job, and no one else is hiring round here, I can tell you. So, don't work if you don't like. It's all the same to me. There's plenty more who want a job if you don't.'

Noki called, 'Hey, tell us, where's the Super, huh? Where is he? Ask him, Cousin Jack, ask him where the Super is. I want to hear it from him, not from this filth.'

'Yes, we want to talk to the Super,' said Red Sven.

'That's right, we want the Super, the Super!' shouted Waterboer, who had accompanied his Griqua labourers to the meeting. They picked up his cry, demanding that the man be brought to them. Others joined in, and soon every person gathered raised their voice in anger. With the mix of accents, the beating of feet and clapping of hands, in a crowd of several thousand, the word became nonsensical, changed to a strange babble of 'Zoomah, zoomah, zoomah!'

Reid put up his hands. 'Now, calm down, boys, calm down. The Super isn't here. He's away making sure the mine gets reopened. He's doing all this for you. He's helping you.'

The bandaged miner shouted, 'Helping us? I heard he's on holiday hunting Cape buffalo.'

Someone replied, 'What's he want that for? He's already got a buffalo for a wife.'

'And warthogs for daughters.'

Laughter broke out, a muffled flow at first, but then it waved on through the crowd, rising in volume, until heads rolled back, mouths widened, teeth were bared. It was the laughter of insult and anger.

Reid tried again. 'Listen, listen, the Super is organising a picnic for when the flowers come. A train trip, and there'll be food and the flowers as a treat after everything that's happened, you know. And you kaffirs won't be forgotten. All the leftover food will be donated to the settlement.'

The laughter stopped, the teeth still bared.

'Are we ants to be sent underground with crumbs?' Noki said. 'Is that what we are? Is it? Is that all we are?'

The crowd began to roar. They raised their fists, jostled forward.

'Keep back, keep back!' Reid shouted, pulling out his pistol and firing in the air. 'You sons of bitches, I've told you: work or don't. I don't care.' He jumped off the mound, fleeing across to his hut.

They did not disperse once Reid had left. They fretted amongst themselves, their ire mounting.

Noki stood apart with the Cousin Jack and some others. 'This is insanity on the Company's part,' the Cornishman said. 'We can't work like that.'

'What can we do?' said Red Sven, shrugging his shoulders as so many around him were doing. 'We can make threats, but what do they mean when we have no power?'

Tengo nodded. 'It's like Reid says, we can only work or not work. There are no other options.'

'But what if we all come together, all of us, miners and workers, if we all come together and use our numbers as a way to negotiate?'

They had not seen the man arrive, but Waterboer spoke now: 'Did I hear you correctly, Mr Tregowning? Are you proposing a strike?'

'Not a strike exactly. I'm talking about negotiations, where we all express our grievances. Peaceful negotiations.'

'Peaceful? What good is that?' said Zamikhaya.

'Look, I've seen it happen before, in a mine I worked in America. We held talks – peaceful ones – and had some good results. It might be worth a try, don't you think?' He glanced at those who had been listening.

Waterboer held his hands together. 'The Lord has spoken to me. He has told me that the Griqua people must join the strike. He will guide us.'

'Piss off, you. Go back to your preaching. You know nothing about mining, so stay out of this,' said Zamikhaya. 'We don't want you here.'

'Quiet,' said Noki. He had remained unsettled since his conversation in the wilderness with the boy; disturbed by Solomon's need for action, his energy to make something happen without waiting for others. Noki's feebleness in the face of what his brother had suffered, in the face of what he himself had always accepted as a reasonable way of living and working, had been laid bare to him. That

183

weakness could not continue. And though he did not seek violence or revenge, he would find a way to force things to change, if he could. 'How do we get everyone to agree to this?' he said to Tregowning. 'It's a lot to ask and I don't think they'll like it. They'll be afraid.'

'I understand that, believe me, but all we can do is speak to them and see what they have to say. There are many angry people here, people who want to be heard. We can only try.'

All at once the crowd began to shift uncertainly. They muttered and shuffled, some of them attempting to move forward, others to retreat. Ten armed men, Company men all, had come over the flattened mine heaps and positioned themselves in a semi-circle facing the gathering. They did not point their rifles, but stood, hands on hips, weapons slung over their shoulders.

'They mean to frighten us,' said Tregowning.

'Come,' said Noki, 'spread the word. Tengo, Zamikhaya, tell everyone to move away from the mine. We'll meet at the koppie at the centre of town. Waterboer, did you hear? Tell your men too. And Solomon, run now quickly and let everyone know that you can see, tell them all. We must act now.'

The boy glanced up at him, gave a quick nod. 'I'm going.'

The message went from mouth to mouth, and the workers began to move slowly towards the central koppie a quarter of a mile away. It was little more than a pile of boulders, but it was onto this that Noki and his companions climbed as they waited for the crowd to re-form. Many pushed their way to the foot of the koppie, but there were those too who stood at the outskirts, their arms crossed in suspicion, wondering what this meeting would prove to be.

Noki began, 'We have come here from different tribes, different countries. We have come for one reason only. To work in the mines and make a living so that we can feed our families. Our brothers died while doing that, dying for no reason other than the Company's carelessness. Where is the honour in that? Do we want the same for ourselves? Do we want to die in a collapse that we have only just escaped? Do we want our families to starve because of the shit they want to pay us? If we agree to their terms, we'll be lucky to come out of the mine alive, lucky not to go hungry. Is that what you want for yourselves, for your families, your children?'

'No, no!' came the reply.

'The Company runs everything here. It says, "Eat now, work now, piss now, die now." But it never says, "Speak now." How long can we let it take everything from us? Now is the time to come together and speak with one voice. Now is the time to tell the Company that we reject their offer, that we will negotiate with them as equals, no less than that.'

Men brought fists skywards, shouted.

'Tomorrow, then, we meet here at this koppie. And we do not go underground until we have spoken to the Super. We do not work until we have negotiated better pay and better conditions. Are we agreed?'

'Yes, yes!' came the cry. They would not be kept down any longer. They would rise.

Dawn had not yet broken and already the bouldered koppie was surrounded by strikers. Mostly men had come, but there were among them a few women and children. They spread out from the hillock, seated on the ground, talking amongst themselves, some of them smiling, some laughing, others wrapping their arms around their near-nakedness in the cold morning air. The tribal groups had chosen to attend the meeting in their traditional dress: wraps of animal skin, beads and metal decorations, different items of formal significance. They carried, too, the ceremonial weapons of their tribes: spears, knobkieries, tall whips and shields. Amongst the white miners, similar attempts had been made. Several Scottish men donned kilts, reeking of must from having been stored away for years. Red Sven wore a blue waistcoat, embroidered with flowers. A few Irishmen had found a tattered flag of the Green Harp and carried that above them. One Cornishman's wife had taken an old sheet and flour sack, fashioning for herself the traditional outfit of the bal maiden with gook and long apron. Some, who had no items of ancestral value, had dug out tintypes of family members, both dead and alive, and planted them in the bands of their hats. Others, of all races, simply came in clothes separate from their work uniform, showing that they had no intention of going underground that day.

By sunrise five men had been elected to represent the case of the miners. They were Tregowning, Noki, Waterboer, a heavily muscled Zulu named Bhekumbuso, and a tall Herero, Kilus. Five was the number, it was agreed, because while many mouths could sing and chant at one time, they could not all talk at once and expect to be heard. Five only would speak for the people and lead the negotiations.

Singing followed. It was begun by a few of the Xhosa men, a traditional song from their homeland, no more than a gentle tune about the high mountains and blue sky above. Though it was not known to everyone, soon it was being sung across the expanse of the valley, with makeshift lyrics to the borrowed tune. But by late afternoon what had begun in peace had turned to restiveness. The songs had grown louder, angrier, had become chants of war. Most of the men now stood, their weapons raised above their heads. Why had no one come to speak to them? Why had no one come?

Yet, when at last Reid did arrive, accompanied by his armed guard, each of the strikers knelt down at once, placing their weapons on the ground, or if they carried none, simply put their empty hands on the earth. They knelt, not in deference to the mine boss but out of respect for the negotiations and the deputation of men that parted from the crowd and approached Reid.

Noki spoke first. 'Our case is simple. We want to be listened to. We want to talk about decent wages and decent conditions. We would like to talk to the Super.'

'And who are you, kaffir, to make demands?'

'It is not a demand, it is a request. A request shared by every man that you see here.'

Tregowning said, 'We ask only to be heard.'

'I should have known you'd be involved in this, Cornish. You're wasting your time. I've told you, the Super isn't here. He's not coming.'

'We will wait,' Noki called after the man as he walked away. 'Who is more like stone than us? We will wait. We know how.'

By late evening Hull walked through the mass of strikers. There were jeers and hisses as he passed, men spat in his direction – they understood the magistrate and Company to be one. It was he who had allowed prisoners to be tortured and killed, he who was keeping their bodies under lock and key while he performed some sort of witchcraft on them.

When he reached the delegation on the koppie, Hull shook hands with each of the five men. 'I have come to warn you to be careful. Reid has asked me to give him use of my constables. I have refused. As long as the strike is peaceful there is no need for violence. But he has sent to Okiep for men.'

'We have also sent to Okiep to persuade them to join the strike,' Tregowning said.

'You don't understand. These are armed men he has sent for. He is gathering an army against you.'

'We understand,' Noki said.

'By God, let there be no killing, I beg you. Do not provoke them.'

'We want only to talk. If we are heard then there will be no need of violence in any form. I promise you that we are not seeking it.'

'Keep it so, I beg you. So much has already been lost here.'

'I am telling you, there will be no bloodshed from us. You can pass that on to Reid if you like. Tell him that we are waiting. Either he brings the Super to us or he takes us to the Super. We're waiting.'

'I will pass the message on, as you ask. Much good it may do you. I wish you all the best.' He shook hands with each man again and climbed back down the koppie, towards the mine boss's shack.

Long afterwards, once Reid's curses had stopped ringing in his ears, he posted himself at the door of the Residency. The masses had stretched as far as the fence-posts, and he watched them now, trembling where he stood, recalling the visions he had had on board the *Namaqua*. Of weaponed savages coming towards him with spears and arrows. Of bloodied carcasses and war cries. He was convinced that he could smell blood, that it was all around, as though it were being carried by the clouds themselves. There would be blood, he was certain of that. Blood and death, and he had no weapon at all. Nothing but the hope that his position might have some value, might mean anything at all, and allow him to reason with Reid. It was Reid he feared most, Reid and his army that would arrive at any minute.

He chewed an unsteady finger, biting away the urge to lock the house, to shutter the windows, to drink down a tumbler of brandy. He wanted to hide behind his armchair, up the chimney, under the bed, anywhere at all. But he remained at his post, his stomach fluttering, the smell of blood in his nose.

On the morning of the third day, Reid walked out in front of the crowd as he had done on the first, accompanied by guards. But on this day the number of armed men had multiplied, so that two score or more of them formed a wide arc in front of the crowd. He kept his left hand in his jacket pocket, fondling a slip of paper until it softened and split. It was a telegraph message, bearing instructions from the Super. *Shoot down the dastardly criminals if need be. The mine must reopen.*

'Your time on the koppie is over,' he called, illustrating his words with a wave of his right hand at the armed men. 'There is no more time for waiting. It is the same as before. Work or don't work. There will be no negotiations, no talking to the Super. Now, start dispersing or you will be made to move.'

The strikers rose from where they had been kneeling. They lifted their weapons from the ground and brought them up into the air, shouting. They paid no heed to the rifles being lowered, the pistols being cocked. Perhaps there was a feeling of invincibility in their numbers; they were many. They had come together against the Company, making it suddenly small. The Company was nothing. Nothing at all. They were everything.

'Move away!' Reid yelled.

But they shouted back at this insignificant man who no longer scared them, who did not even have the ability to comprehend their strength. It was all fury now. All rage. There was no more space for talking. Only noise would suffice, and the miners struck up chants that carried far beyond the valley.

Still at his post, a blanket around his shoulders, Hull sat in the doorway, his back numb against the doorframe. His eyes rolled with lack of sleep, his ears thrummed, and it was with difficulty that he rose upon hearing Reid's voice. He observed the mounting anger of the crowd, and his fears of the previous day returned. Again he felt ill, his stomach loose. He looked around the valley, at the sun still low, the interminably grey sky, the flattened mine heaps and the surrounding hills, all echoing with the voices of the strikers. It seemed incapable of containing their anger, this narrow valley, this ring of stone. The rage burst upwards, tumbled over mountains, threatened its way into further valleys, across the veld, into burrows and onto peaks.

He had not seen Reid's army arriving, though come they certainly had, no doubt avoiding the Okiep Road with purpose. He glanced towards that road now, wondering whether another flank might yet arrive to hem in the miners from behind. There was indeed some movement a little way off, faint in the mist. It was sure to be more armed men, approaching fast. But soon it became clear that there was only one horse and cart. The horse was unruly, baulking at the noise of the mob, attempting to bolt as the driver whipped it without success. It whinnied in fright, reared up. The driver was thrown to the ground, and the horse jerked forward, galloping away with the cart still attached.

It was Mrs McBride, Hull realised. She wore her veil, but it had come adrift in the fall. He could make out her alarm at the chanting men ahead. He ran across, shouting to be heard as he helped her to her feet, 'Good God! Why have you come?'

'I – I heard they wanted my father. He is not here and he will not come, and so I came. Someone had to, didn't they? Someone must hear them if he won't.'

'But can't you see it isn't safe? You must turn back.'

All at once there came the crack of rifle fire. Shot after shot, ringing out against the valley's boulders. Screams

191

followed. People began to flee. Those nearest the Residency pushed past Hull and Mrs McBride, knocking them to the ground in their flight. They tried to rise, fell again. Hull took her hands, was able to pull her up, to lift her over the fence and make for the cottage at the far end of the grounds.

'What is happening?' she sobbed. 'Oh God, why are they shooting?'

Hull unlocked the door and pushed her inside. 'Why are you here?' he said again. 'What were you thinking?'

'My father—'

'Don't you know what manner of man your father is? Your presence here can be nothing but an insult to them. Can't you see that?'

'Not me,' she cried. 'Do not say that. I'm not like him. He is nothing to me, I detest him, detest him! Don't you know that, after everything I've told you?'

Hull made her sit on the dusty wooden floor.

'Please, let me help.' She made to rise, her hand slipping, coming down to land on the torso of one of the desiccated bodies that still filled the cottage. She shrank away, began to scream, but Hull placed a hand over her mouth, hushed her gently. 'Do not be afraid. They cannot harm you.'

Her eyes were wild as she scanned the room, but she did not call out when he removed his hand, only said, 'I can't stay here, don't make me stay here amongst all this.'

'You must. Keep hidden and quiet. Do not move from this place until I come for you.'

He locked the door and ran towards the firing, his body hunched over, his hands covering his head. He passed dead men, wounded men, but he did not pause until he reached the mine boss's shed. 'Make them stop, goddammit! You're shooting fleeing men. For God's sake, you're shooting them in the back.'

'I have my orders,' Reid said, keeping his hand in his pocket, the telegram no more than a ball of pulp.

There had been no place in the strikers' plans for violent action, and they had taken flight under the attack. They escaped into houses, climbed onto roofs. Many fled to the mine, and hid in tunnels that had been dug during the rescue. Some twenty ran in the direction of the smelter and found themselves cornered in a low area with boulders too large and smooth to scale. Behind, they were stalked by three armed men, who, despite the workers' raised hands, shot them down where they stood.

Only a few, unwilling to see their brothers murdered, turned against the tide. Zamikhaya called to Solomon, told him to grab what weapon he could and follow himself and four others. They sought Reid above all else. He was the agent of the massacre, he had caused this to happen. Seeing the approaching men, the mine boss scrambled into his shed, pushed a desk and stool in front of the door. He had long since unloaded his pistol and was without protection. 'We'll get you, Reid,' said Zamikhaya. 'We're coming for you.' They shoved at the sides of the hut, tried to break holes in the wood with their knobkieries and spears. One of them lit a match, set it to the building, and they cheered as the wood smoked wetly.

Both Noki and Tregowning were still on the koppie. Both saw the group start the fire, saw as the man lurched out coughing, his hands raised. But it was Tregowning who was first down the boulders, who ran towards Zamikhaya and his men. 'Stop this! Stop! You cannot do this!' He tried to grab their weapons with his unbound hand, to move them off and allow Reid to escape.

Noki was slow behind him, hampered by fallen men, by a guard who had lost his rifle and attacked with a long spear that he had pilfered from a corpse. A tight circle had formed near the boss's shed, Reid and the Cousin Jack lost within it. Noki could see raised arms, saw them come down again. 'Wait,' he called, but already it was over, and Solomon was stepping away, the machete he held red with blood. The boy gave a shriek, lunged forward into the battling crowd, landing on the back of one of the armed men from Okiep. He brought the blade down on the man's neck, riding the body as it fell.

The others had moved on too, and Noki arrived alone to find that the mine boss had been decapitated. Beside him lay the Cousin Jack. His limbs had been removed from his body, his skull split open.

He found Solomon leaning against the stables, the body of a Company man beside him. The boy was covered in blood, and clutched the machete between both hands.

'How many is it that you've killed?' said Noki.

'I don't know. Ten. A hundred.'

'Come,' he said, taking the boy's arm. 'Put that down now. It's time for us to go. We cannot stay. We must go.'

He dropped the weapon, and all at once became small, a child. 'My mother,' he said.

'You must forget your mother for now.'

'My father.'

'Your father is dead.'

'I was going to be a man and go underground and find him.'

'You cannot do that now. We must go.'

'Are we going home?'

'Yes, to the home that has been left to us.'

He held the boy's hand and led him away, out across the veld towards the hills and mountains that separated Springbokfontein from all else.

Hull unlocked the door. He had brought with him Ned and two horses. Mrs McBride had remained where he had left her, her skirts pulled up to her chin. He knelt beside her, held out his hand. 'It is better for you to go home now. Ned will make sure that you get there safely. You will have to go the long way, I'm afraid, away from the road. Once you are home you had best stay indoors; you and your mother and sister and little George. Do not go outside. And do not return to Springbokfontein until all of this is well over, do you understand?'

She nodded as he helped her to her feet. Then, 'Have many died?' she asked.

'It has been a massacre.'

She kept hold of his arm, letting go only as he lifted her onto one of the horses. 'Mr Hull, William…' she began, looking down into his face, but she said no more after that, turning away from him in tears. He stepped back, sick with what he wished to speak, saying instead, 'Ride with care, Mrs McBride. Go on, Ned.'

Afterwards he strode across to the Residency. He packed his trunks, clearing his drawers and wardrobe in haste, before dragging them onto the veranda. He locked the door and walked the short distance to the hotel, stepping around the blood-soaked earth, tracks where bodies had been dragged. Three times he had to ring the bell at the reception desk, three times call for Mr Flatley, the landlord. When the man appeared, Hull asked to rent a room and for his things to be brought over.

'Can't fetch 'em now,' Flatley said. 'We'll send someone for 'em later, when it's safe. But you can go up so long and rest.'

Hull went up the crooked stairs to a bedroom and lay down on the hard cot for a moment. He got up again and looked out through the window at the street where bodies were being piled into carts. After a time, he removed his jacket and tie, lay down once more. His hands trembled, and he pushed them in beneath his thighs in an attempt to still them. Again he rose, called down the hall for a jug of water and a basin. When they were brought, he washed his hands, his face, his neck. The water coloured to pink, and he wondered how he had come to have so much blood on him.

He went down for breakfast without having slept. He had been unable to close his eyes, seeing before him too much of what had passed. The army of Company men had walked amongst the fallen. Those who were alive, who lifted their heads, who called out, had been silenced. Guards stood on the backs of anyone who tried to crawl away, punched the ones that rose. Before his eyes living men had passed away, dying as they asked for mercy. Shots had rung out, men slain where they lay.

'Move away please, Mr Magistrate,' an armed man had said when Hull tried to intervene. 'This is Company business. Your meddling is not advised. Go home and lock the door until you are wanted.'

Afterwards they had torn through the settlement like rabid dogs, setting fire to shacks, shooting people as they fled from burning homes.

Mr Flatley gossiped over Hull as he set the table. 'Crikey, that was a business yesterday. Never been so scared in my life. The wife and I were hiding in a cupboard. Thank God for the Super's men, eh, else we might all've been dead. He's back now, you know. Came back last night, I heard from one of those guards this morning when I went out to inspect the damage. Couple of bullet holes in the wall, but I can easily stop 'em up.'

'You say the Super has returned?'

'So I hear.'

'Then I am in need of a horse at once,' Hull said. 'Send your man to the Company's stables. Tell them to let me have a fast one as I am in great haste. I cannot wait another moment.'

He rode directly for Okiep, where he was dusted off as before, and shown into the Super's private office.

'Ah, Hull,' said Townsend as he looked up from his paperwork. 'You've been a lot of trouble, sir, interfering in every which way. But I hear you are leaving us. Thank God, is all I can say. You've been nothing but a disappointment so far.'

'No, Mr Townsend, you have been misinformed. I am not leaving. I have simply moved out of the Residency. I am done with the Company perks and bribes, that is what I have come to tell you. Here is your key,' he said, laying it on the desk. 'However, I intend to remain magistrate of this region and I will do so without your interference.'

The Super laughed. 'Do you think giving up a few postage stamps makes you a hero? In whose eyes, I ask you? In whose eyes? It changes nothing.'

'It may be nothing, but the law is something. I will find you culpable somehow, whether for the murders in the jail, the mine collapse or the strikers shot down. One way or another I will see that justice comes to this mining region.'

'Do what you like. The Company is far greater than you and much stronger than the law.'

'The pebble may dislodge the boulder, Mr Townsend.'

'Yes, you are a pebble, as you say. An annoying pebble in my shoe that I can throw out at any moment, don't believe that I can't.'

'I am here to stay, Mr Townsend. I shall not waver. That is all I have to say for the present. Good day.'

Hull showed himself out. He lingered momentarily in the hallway, hoping perhaps to see Mrs McBride, but she did not appear and he left the house wondering whether he would see her again. He closed the low garden gate, adjusted his hat, considering whether he might write to her.

'Mr Hull,' came a whisper.

He looked up in surprise, turned to left and right, but could see no one nearby. It came again, and this time he saw Mrs McBride motioning to him from the side of the house. He walked towards her, began to speak, but 'Not here,' she said and moved off into the veld that lay beyond, stopping only once she had come to the large thorn tree that grew there.

'We shan't be seen here,' she said. 'I wanted to say that I was unfair to you before, Mr Hull.'

'No.'

'I was. I have always known what my father is. I knew it and I did nothing about it except run away.' She shook her head and looked up at him. 'I apologise for what I said to you and I wish to thank you for the care you took of me yesterday. You are a fine man, truly, the finest I know. I did not mean what I said before about... well, all those things. Will you shake hands?'

'Of course. It is all forgotten.'

'I was hoping—' he began, but 'I am leaving,' she said. 'We all are. Mama and Kitty and George. Only Father will stay here now. We are being sent away on the next ship. It is no longer safe for us.'

'Where will you go?'

'First to Cape Town, then we catch a steamer to London. From there I believe we go somewhere in the north of England, to an uncle who has a manufacturing business.'

'So far? I had hoped... I had thought... after everything, I had thought perhaps that you and I...'

'So much has happened. How can we ever go back to that journey on the mule train or the day we spent together digging for frogs? It is not possible.'

'There is no need to go back. Let us go only forward,' he said, reaching out for her hand. 'What I mean to say is, Mrs McBride, Iris, I admire you greatly. I – I – you must know that I love you. You must know that I wish to share my life with you. I beg you, do not leave.'

She closed her eyes for a moment, gave a strained smile. 'I must think of George, no matter what my own wishes are, it is he that I must consider. I have no money,

Mr Hull. We are dependent on my father's generosity. I am, I can hardly bear to say it, reliant on him to ensure that George's future is one that is wholly separate from the world of mining. I cannot rob him of that opportunity. I cannot allow him to remain here and become one of these men ruined by the industry.'

Hull removed his hat. He twisted the brim, looked down at it. 'I understand what you are saying, and believe me, I would dearly like to leave this place, Iris, to take you and George wherever in the world you wish to go, but I cannot. I have much to repair here. There is so much that is corrupt and poisonous in mining, as you warned me once before. I have made so many errors, and now I begin to know my duty. Though I cannot say how long it may take to have the law work in favour of the weak in this place, I will do what I can to ensure that it does.'

'Do you honestly believe that you can fix what has happened here?'

'I must try.'

'Then you are right to stay and I would not ask you to do otherwise.'

He took her other hand, pulled her towards him. 'When all of this is over and everything has been set to rights, I will come to you. It won't matter where you are. I will find you, in England or elsewhere. I will come.'

She leant forward and kissed his cheek, before removing one of her hands from his, and placing it on the trunk of the thorn tree. 'Do you know what they say about this place? They say that a Hottentot once stood here and said "Wait for me" to his beloved. She waited and waited, but he never came back. The tree grew to shade her from the sun and rain as she waited. Now she is buried beneath it, still waiting.'

Weeks later Noki and Solomon climbed over the rise and looked out at the new city of promise that was before them. They had reached the gold-mining town of the Witwatersrand, a vast expanse of canvas tents, of upturned earth, of timber and rope, picks and spades. Thousands of people moved amongst the mounds and hollows, each earning his keep in one way or another. Their faces hard, Noki and the boy began their descent, hopeful of work that would take them yet again down into the belly of the earth.

Author's Notes and Acknowledgements

While the town of Springbokfontein (now known as Springbok) and the Cape Copper Mining Company (later the Cape Copper Company) and Namaqua Copper Company did exist, the events represented in this book are fictional. For the history of these companies and the copper mining district of Namaqualand, I am grateful for John M. Smalberger's invaluable *Aspects of the History of Copper Mining in Namaqualand 1846–1931* (1975). It was this book which first drew me to the subject matter for this novel and which fuelled it throughout the research and writing periods.

Inspiration for the character of Hull had its inception when I encountered the magistrate William Charles Scully in Smalberger's book. However, the description of Hull's experiences was further influenced upon reading Scully's *Unconventional Reminiscences* (first published as *Reminiscences of a South African Pioneer* and *Further Reminiscences of a South African Pioneer* in 1913). It must be said that Scully was an adventurer and self-made man. All of Hull's weaknesses are his own. In a chapter about his brief magistracy in Namaqualand, Scully writes of his horrific encounters with a jailer he names Berwick (but who, in his correspondence, is identified by his true name of Genricks). Genricks' torture, murder and poisoning of prisoners is based in fact, but the character and events have been fictionalised here, as have those relating to Dr Fox, the Super and the trained lunatic, all of whom are mentioned in Scully's *Unconventional Reminiscences*.

During my research I also read, amongst many other sources, two journalistic books regarding the Marikana Massacre of 16 August 2012: *Marikana: A View from the Mountain* and a *Case to Answer* (2013 – revised edition) and *We are Going to Kill Each Other Today: The Marikana Story* (2013). I turned to these books for information, guidance and insight because, if nothing else, *Upturned Earth* exists as a comment on the history of commercial mining in South Africa – the exploitation, conditions and corruption that began in the 1850s and continue to the present.

I would like to thank the following people and organisations for their assistance and involvement in their different ways during the research and writing of this book: Esmarie Jennings, Juliano Paccez, the Paccez family, Victoria Caceres, Giovanni Agnoloni, Sally Altschuller, Peter and Gitte Rannes, the Hald Hovedgaard Residency near Viborg in Denmark, André Krüger, Tochukwu Okafor, and the Arts and Culture Trust of South Africa for funding one of my research trips to Springbok.

THE AUTHOR

Karen Jennings was born in Cape Town in 1982. She has Masters degrees in both English Literature and Creative Writing from the University of Cape Town and a PhD in Creative Writing from the University of KwaZulu-Natal.

Holland Park Press has published four of Karen's previous books: her debut novel *Finding Soutbek* in 2012, which was shortlisted for the inaugural Etisalat Prize for Literature 2013 and has been translated into French: *Les oubliés du Cap*, Editions de L'Aube, 2017; a short story collection *Away from the Dead* in 2014; *Travels with My Father*, an autobiographical novel, in 2016; and in 2018, her first full poetry collection, *Space Inhabited by Echoes*.

Karen currently lives in Brazil.

More information is available from
https://www.hollandparkpress.co.uk/jennings

Holland Park Press is a privately-owned independent company publishing literary fiction: novels, novellas, short stories; and poetry. It was founded in 2009. It is run by brother and sister, Arnold and Bernadette Jansen op de Haar, who publish an author not just a book. Holland Park Press specialises in finding new literary talent by accepting unsolicited manuscripts from authors all year round and by running competitions. It has been successful in giving older authors a chance to make their debut and in raising the profile of Dutch authors in translation.

To

Learn more about Karen Jennings
Discover other interesting books
Read our unique Anglo-Dutch magazine
Find out how to submit your manuscript
Take part in one of our competitions

Visit www.hollandparkpress.co.uk
Bookshop: http://www.hollandparkpress.co.uk/category/all/
Holland Park Press in the social media:
http://www.twitter.com/HollandParkPres
http://www.facebook.com/HollandParkPress
http://www.linkedin.com/company/holland-park-press
http://www.youtube.com/user/HollandParkPress